THE STORY THAT BROUGHT ME HERE

THE STORY THAT BROUGHT ME HERE
TO ALBERTA FROM EVERYWHERE

EDITED BY LINDA GOYETTE

BRINDLE
& GLASS

Library and Archives Canada Cataloguing in Publication
The story that brought me here : to Alberta from everywhere / Linda Goyette, editor.

ISBN 978-1-897142-34-9

1. Canadian literature (English)—Alberta. 2. Canadian literature (English)—21st century.
3. Alberta—Literary collections. I. Goyette, Linda, 1955-
PS8255.A5S76 2008   C810.8'0327123   C2008-903088-5

Cover image: istockphoto.com

  Canada Council   Conseil des Arts   Canadian   Patrimoine
for the Arts   du Canada   Heritage   canadien

Brindle & Glass is pleased to acknowledge the financial support to its publishing
program from the Government of Canada through the Book Publishing Industry
Development Program (BPIDP) and the Canada Council for the Arts.

Brindle & Glass Publishing
www.brindleandglass.com

Brindle & Glass is committed to protecting the environment and to the responsible use
of natural resources. This book is printed on 100% post-consumer recycled and
ancient-forest-friendly paper. For more information please visit www.oldgrowthfree.com.

1   2   3   4   5   11   10   09   08

PRINTED AND BOUND IN CANADA

To writers, everywhere,
and to the Edmonton Public Library

ズ ズ ズ

CONTENTS

LINDA GOYETTE
The Story That Brought Me Here

You are about to meet thirty-six writers and storytellers who left everything they loved to move north of nowhere.

Well, Alberta might as well have been nowhere. Few of these people knew anything about the province when they arrived here from distant points on the globe. That's not quite true. They knew Alberta was a province in western Canada, rich with oil and the jobs that the oil industry pumps out of the ground. They knew about the Canadian Rockies. They knew winter here would be colder than any season they had ever experienced, or imagined. Everything else was a discovery.

War shoved some of these people in Alberta's direction. It brought Mohammed AL-Nassar, Jalal Barzanji and Sabah Tahir from Iraq; Athiann Makuach Garang from Sudan; Theresa Saffa from Sierra Leone; Marsh Hoke and Gary Garrison from the United States; Thuc Cong and Nhan Thi Lu from Vietnam; A. K. Rashid from Afghanistan; and Chantal Hitayezu from Burundi and Rwanda.

Love for a good man lured Therezinha França Kennedy from a university in Brazil, June Smith-Jeffries from an optician's office in the American south and Shabnam Sukhdev from a promising film career in India.

Love for a beloved family brought Patricia López de Vloothuis from Mexico, and Comfort Adesuwa Ero and Ikponwosa "I. K." Ero from Nigeria. Rita Espeschit thought more about her daughter Alice's future than her own when she came here from Brazil.

The University of Alberta drew Nduka Otiono from Nigeria, Yi Li from China, Peter Midgley from South Africa and Augustine Marah from Sierra Leone. Alberta's mountains called to Wilma Rubens in Australia, and she couldn't resist them. The Rockies also helped Sangmok Lee contend with his longing for Korea.

A better job, or the sweet promise of success, enticed Sudhir Jain from Libya, Vladimir Silva from Peru, Monika Igali from Hungary via New Brunswick, Mansoor Ladha from Tanzania via Ontario, Mary Cavill from England, Mieke Alexander from the Netherlands, and Nung Jai Park from Korea. Reinekke Lengelle came here only because her father insisted; she returned to Europe as soon as she could . . . but came back.

Brian Brennan left Ireland on a lark. Ahmui Cheong left Singapore to explore the world and visited Alberta several times before deciding to move here. Magdalena Witkowski left Poland for an adventure. Father Basil Solounias, an Orthodox priest, came here from Lebanon via New York to care for a congregation.

Some of these writers unpacked rough manuscripts from their suitcases, as well as books they had published in the languages of the world. All brought stories from home that travel with them wherever they go. Did they intend to stay long in Alberta? I didn't ask. Staying, like life, just happens. What did they lose when they left the nations of their birth? What gifts did they bring? You are about to find out.

Long ago, in Alberta's other lifetime, before oil made the province rich, an Icelandic farmer came here to scrape a farm from the unforgiving land. Exhausted at night, he would return to his desk to write poetry. Stephan Stephansson published more that two thousand pages of verse—all in Icelandic—in his seventy-one years. He is revered in Iceland to this day yet barely known in Canada, the country where he lived for much of his life. In a farmhouse near Markerville, Alberta, in 1891, Stephansson wrote a poem that echoes through this book, and hovers over the shoulders of its writers. It speaks of the in-between place where all writers live and the unique displacement of those who continue to write in their mother tongue when they move to a new country. Here is a fragment of "The Exile," in Paul Sigurdson's translation.

Even here the lingering twilight
Warms the meadows green,
Even here the streams meander
Rolling hills between;
Here the waves in lyric singing
Break along the strand
Yet somehow it has come upon me
I've no fatherland.

The Story That Brought Me Here emerged from a wish, a library, one poet's unbending conviction, and the friendship of many writers.

The wish pushed its way into my imagination one day when I was interviewing citizens for *Edmonton In Our Own Words*, a collective memoir of the city's history, published in 2004. Intriguing people were telling me rich, layered stories about the countries they had left behind, and I was supposed to gently interrupt and ask them about their lives in Edmonton. "I wish I could ask about the place where this story began," I grumbled to myself. "That would be an interesting book." A wish took hold and would not let go.

Enter the Edmonton Public Library. I had been working in the downtown library since 2002, first as an itinerant story-collector and later as the Writer in Residence in 2007. I love the place. With the encouragement and support of the library's staff, I began to search for the migration stories of recent newcomers. I found an interesting photograph of stacks of suitcases, spilling their contents at the side of a road: a women's dress, a saxophone. We posted the photograph and a notice on the library website and circulated the flyer. *Did you come to Alberta from another corner of the world? Are you a writer who would like to publish your work in Canada? We are seeking compelling stories and poetry for a new book to be published in the fall of 2006, and for a new collection of local writing in the World Languages section of the Edmonton Public Library.* At NorQuest College, I asked ESL students to contribute stories in the language of their choice. They prepared a booklet, "Arrival Stories," and read their work at a special CBC forum and broadcast. I searched for newcomers around Alberta I might interview in more depth and wrote an article for *Alberta Views* magazine, full of their stories, partly to challenge Canada's self-satisfied definition of itself as a welcoming nation. Then a wish took flight, soaring in a new direction.

Local writers began to arrive at the library with books and manuscripts in languages other than English. Many had lived in Canada for a considerable amount of time and continued to write and publish poetry, short stories, plays, novels, screenplays, and journalism in distant places. Others were just beginning to write in English, or in another language, and knew nothing about how to find a translator, an editor, an arts grant or a publisher in Canada. Some were gifted storytellers who wanted to find a way to offer their oral tradition to a new country. Stephan Stephannson would have recognized them as kindred spirits. Like him, most are unknown as writers, invisible as artists, in their adopted nation.

A wider circle of writers found a home at the library, and we met on Sunday afternoons for conversations. We invited published writers, editors, publishers, and grants officers to talk about the way things work in the literary community in Alberta and in the rest of Canada. Sometimes we talked quietly, sometimes fiercely, about the way things don't work at all: about literary cliques, racism, unfair rules, and doors that open for some writers and slam shut for others. We read one another's work. We encouraged one another. We became friends. A collection of stories and poems began to take shape as a manuscript. Then a wish flew across the North Saskatchewan river and encountered a poet's conviction.

I had wanted to meet Iman Mersal for a long time. She is a poet who has lived in Edmonton for a decade while publishing to international acclaim. Born and educated in Egypt, she teaches at the University of Alberta. Few people in the city have read her avant-garde poetry because she writes in Arabic and the translations of her work have appeared primarily in other countries. If Albertans know about her, they remember the wretched story of a numbskull thief who ransacked her home in the summer of 2007, stealing her laptop computer and a bag that contained backup copies of two years of work. Her spirit survived the ordeal, and this fall she will publish her first collection in English, *These Are Not Oranges, My Love*, with a New York publisher.

I asked Iman to contribute a poem to the anthology, and she politely declined. In the way of explanation, she invited me to a lecture she was about to give at the university, titled "Eliminating Diasporic Identities." She was preparing an important paper for PMLA, the journal of the Modern Languages Association. Was I interested? Well, not really, but on a whim, I went.

It was one of those afternoons you remember for a long time, a cold day when stale ideas are challenged and certainties go flying all to hell. Iman spoke eloquently about the way foreign-born writers are pushed and prodded into rigid categories when they move from another nation to

North America. A story template is waiting for them whether they know it or not. They are expected to pull on the overcoat of the exiled writer, the immigrant writer, the ethnic writer, the oppressed writer who has finally discovered freedom of expression in a democratic society. What if they only want to be a writer? "The burden," she said, "is the enormous number of identities imposed by others, without one's permission or consent." She spoke from her own experience:

> What does it mean to be a writer who writes in Arabic, who grew up in an Arabic-speaking Islamic environment, who came to live in North America but who recognizes herself neither as an Arab American writer, nor as a writer of colour, nor as a Muslim writer? Who are you when you find yourself constantly participating in labeled activities, with no way of avoiding their labels, as when you are invited to read poetry in a "reading by women of colour"? Or when you give an interview about writing which is published—to your surprise—in a magazine's special issue on "Islamisme"? Who are you when you can no longer be received simply as a writer in Arabic?

In short, she wanted nothing to do with a book of "immigrant writing." But this book is a conversation about a journey from Somewhere Else to Here, I protested; a book is not a ghetto. I did see her point. Labels are prisons. I understood her refusal to contribute to an anthology that would inevitably be defined by some people as a collection of "immigrant writing" rather than as a simple collection of personal stories and poems about the experience of moving from distant places to one small, icy corner of the planet.

If only we could take a crowbar to locked doors and unwanted labels, cliques and categories, and leave their scattered bits on the ground. Couldn't we just tell vivid stories about a birthplace, a departure, a journey, and an arrival? Couldn't we push poems over borders in a Babel of languages? Some questions are universal. Where is home? Where do I belong? What did I leave behind? What will I find here? Where can I be happy?

The writers and storytellers in *The Story That Brought Me Here* speak only for themselves. They do not claim to represent their countries of origin, their cultural communities, or the millions of newcomers who have arrived here through the decades. This is not a Noah's Ark of Alberta's literary traditions, with writers marching two by two, from every nation on the planet. This is not a book about contemporary life in Alberta, either, although at times the authors challenge this society to the core.

Most of the writers and storytellers live in Edmonton, a few are from Calgary, and some are from rural Alberta. Their original stories and poems will be housed in a special collection in the World Languages section of the Stanley Milner Library—in their original languages and in translation. Royalties from the sale of this book will go to PEN Canada, part of an international organization that defends the freedom of expression of writers. Our collective purpose is to nurture the pleasure of reading and to introduce writers and storytellers to Canadian readers who might not know them yet.

We are grateful to Linda Cook and the inspiring staff at the Edmonton Public Library for offering a home to this project for several years and for keeping doors open to all of Edmonton's writers, in all circumstances. We also want to thank the Edmonton Cultural Capital community arts fund for a grant that paid an honorarium to each writer. We are especially grateful to three dedicated translators who assisted contributors to this book: Soheil Najm, Mieun Kwak, and Anna Mioduchowska. We appreciate the hard work of Susan Bright, Shirley Serviss, Rita Espeschit, Barbara Dacks, and Eva Radford who helped some writers with poetic form in English. Shabnam Sukhdev was the project photographer, and an enthusiastic supporter. Other photographers Sangmok Lee, Tracy Kolenchuk, Darren Jacknisky, Marie Sedivy and Faisal Asiff offered generous assistance. I also want to thank Don Bouzek, Yvonne Chiu, Jim Gurnett, John Mahon and the Edmonton Arts Council, Najma Karmali, Michael Phair, Sheineen Nathoo, Mayank Rehani, Venkatesh Shastri, and Allan Chambers for inspiration and support. I am very grateful to Ruth Linka of Brindle & Glass for embracing this project from its first day—she has a beautiful way of creating books out of wishes.

Most of all I want to thank thirty-six individuals who offered a story or a poem to this book, and one individual who would not. They are not immigrant writers. They are writers. Our friendship is a treasure.

Writers Are Stronger Than Armies

My name is Jalal Barzanji, and I am originally from Kurdistan. Many people are unfamiliar with Kurdistan. It is not an independent country. It is the traditional territory of the Kurdish people. We live in Iraq, Syria, Iran, and Turkey, and the borders of these countries have nothing to do with our lives. I am from the part of Kurdistan that has been occupied by Iraq.

I asked my mother about the date of my birth. She told me that it was around the time when the grass was green, and cows were ready to graze in the grassland. That means spring. There was no school in our village. My mother had never been to school, so she only knew the seasons. Although I was born on an unknown day in the spring, in all of my personal documents, my birthday is listed as July 1, 1953. You might find it strange that my wife and two of my brothers have the same birthday. The former dictator, Saddam Hussein, insisted that a quarter of the Iraqi people celebrate their birthday on July 1st to make it easier to send young people for military service. His choice for the day of my birth was for the purpose of war.

I was seven years old when the first school opened in a nearby village, not too far from our house. There was a river between the school and my home that often caused floods during the wintertime. Sometime we would miss classes for a day because of the flooding. Most students would be happy to miss school, but for the children of our village, it was different. Going to school was new. We wanted to go to school every day.

Our little village was a peaceful place between beautiful mountains. It was there I learned about the beauty and simplicity of life. I learned how nature coloured our Earth, how the birds make their nests and find refuge for their babies. There I learned to love beauty in the simple things around us. In this village everything was familiar to me, including the little birds we called *paraselka*, maybe like your sparrows and starlings . . . and the farm animals, the goats, sheep, and cattle.

I thought the sun rose in the nearby mountains, east of my village. I thought the sun set beyond the mountain, west of my village. This small place was the whole world for me. As a child I did not know there was another city or town beyond these mountains.

I had not yet finished the first grade of school when the Iraqi war planes bombed our home and lit everything we ever knew and owned on fire. The people who survived were forced to flee the village and run to a city called Howler. My family ran, too. We had nothing. For my parents, who were farmers, it was a big shock to leave the land they loved, the place they were born.

This big city was like a big exile to them. For me it was difficult, too. I missed my quiet village, my classmates and my teacher. It was a terrible change, but I suddenly realized the world was bigger than our village and I was excited about that. I saw cars for the first time on long and narrow roads. I saw a huge school and many large buildings. It did not take too long for me to adapt to all the changes and become a city boy.

I grew up to love literature. As I grew older and studied in university, I always loved reading the works of the writers from around the world in translation. They inspired me to start writing. I was influenced by the

French poets Baudelaire and Rimbaud, T. S. Eliot, Hemingway, Boris Pasternak, and many others.

At the age of twenty-three, in 1979, I published my first collection of poetry under the title *Dance of the evening snow*. It was well received by Kurdish readers as a new work in a modern style and with a modern vision. I continued writing poetry and articles about beauty, peace, human rights, democracy, love, and freedom. In 1985 I published a second collection of poems. It was three months after that book was published, on a winter evening, when a group of Saddam's soldiers entered my home, blindfolded my eyes and handcuffed me to throw me in jail in my own city. I had committed no crime; I was jailed only because of my poems, my writing, and my freedom of thought. I did not bow to Saddam's regime, and for them, it was a crime.

The conditions in jail were disturbing and inhumane. The cells were incredibly small. Later I moved to a cell built for fifteen people, but forty people were crowded inside. We had thirty-five centimetres marked for each of us as a sleeping space. We could only sleep on our sides. I spent three years in prison, and then I was let out under surveillance.

Life under Saddam's regime was hell at its worst. No one was allowed to live in freedom because one true statement would put your life at risk. I hope to write about everything I experienced and witnessed in jail as part of my prison memoir. I am writing this book this year so that the stories of others will not be forgotten.

In Iraq, under Saddam, everything fell under state control through suffering, blood, and military power. Writers lived in an atmosphere of fear. I managed to publish five books of poetry with great difficulty. Saddam knew that writers and artists refused to follow him. Censorship and the high price of publishing silenced us, but we would not bend to him. For us the cost of free expression was too heavy: jail or even execution. For me, a modern Kurdish citizen and a writer, too, the pain and the price was double. I was pardoned on Saddam's birthday, like many other prisoners, but fear never left me. Outside jail I knew I could expect to go to prison again. I felt like a writer under siege. A free media only grows in a civil, stable society, and in a country where a government believes in a multicultural, democratic system. That does not exist in Iraq to this day.

In 1996, before dawn, I woke up to the sound of Iraqi war planes attacking my city. I heard gunfire. I knew this was a sign that the city would soon be occupied by the army. The screams and fear among people filled the air. Some people were in a frantic state, trying to leave the city. Other people were preparing to fight the regime with small guns against big tanks and planes. They wanted to stop them from entering our city.

I had never used a gun before. My pen was my only weapon to fight for a better world. I decided to leave the country. I had no choice but to leave my wife and three small children behind in Iraq until I could send for them. We found smugglers to help us get into Turkey. In Turkey, again, I paid some money to another person to help me to fly to Ukraine. From there I hoped to enter Sweden to claim refugee status.

However my plan did not work. In the airport at Kiev I was stopped because I did not have a valid visa. I was deported back to Istanbul. Filled with frustration and let down, I had to sleep in the Turkish airport for two nights. In my empty pocket I had a phone number of a Kurdish man who lived in Turkey. He helped me to appeal to the United Nations High Commissioner for Refugees to claim refugee status. First the Canadian embassy accepted me as a true refugee, and later on, they encouraged my family to come out of Iraq to become immigrants to Canada.

This was a hopeful time for us. After all the struggles and disappointments we were happy that Canadians had accepted us into their country. For me and my family it was our dream come true to finally live in a peaceful nation.

Our flight from Turkey to Canada began at 6 AM. We slept one night at the airport in Istanbul until our flight was ready to take off, but during these long hours, we were filled with joy because we knew Canada was opening its door to our family. We had a six-hour wait in Toronto to get to our Edmonton flight. My wife, Sabah, suggested we stay in Toronto because there would be more Kurdish people in the city. I was determined to land in a place where I was destined to go. It was Edmonton, the city chosen for me by the immigration authorities in Turkey. I had never heard of this city before, but I knew it was my place.

We arrived in Edmonton on February 28, 1998, speaking no English, with no money in our pockets. The airline had lost our suitcases. All we had was a huge amount of hope about our new life in Canada.

In the first couple of months, like any other newcomers, we faced many challenges and some disappointments. I think the move was easier for me than some people because I was a writer. As a writer in Kurdistan, I had already learned how to imagine living in places where I had never been. Writing created a mentality for me to be in new places. Writing helped me find my place in Canada.

When I was imprisoned in Iraq, my biggest concern was that I would be separated from my passion for writing, and all the resources to write. I wrote letters on scraps of paper. Later, in Turkey, I was so concerned with my family's horrible living experience, and I was afraid that I would lose touch with my pen. The important part of writing for me has always been the freedom to write beyond rules.

In Canada, I found I had the freedom to write and to look back on my past experiences. But I had no *time* to write because I had to work hard to learn English, find a job, and support my family. I wrote at night, and on weekends, whenever I could. Writing with a new vision was important to me, but I was still constrained until a dream came true.

In the fall of 2006, the famous Canadian writer John Ralston Saul came to Edmonton to speak at LitFest, our literary festival. He asked writers in Edmonton to help oppressed writers who live in exile. A city councillor, Michael Phair, and the writer Todd Babiak invited a committee of citizens to make this happen. In 2007 Edmonton decided to be the first city in Canada to appoint its own PEN Canada Writer in Exile. This appointment will change each year to help new writers.

Receiving the news of this appointment was the greatest moment for me since I came to Canada. The position gives me great joy and makes me proud to be here. The Iraqi government put me in jail because of my writing. In Canada I have been appointed to a position of honour for the same writing. I have had a full year to put all of my time and energy into my work. I write in an office at the Edmonton Public Library, and at the University of Alberta. I am hoping to finish my memoir soon. I am grateful to the people of Edmonton for this opportunity.

When we use our words together, writers are stronger than armies and dictators. When we write, there is no cost in blood or tears. If we defend one another's freedom, we can make the world more peaceful, more beautiful, for everyone. That is our purpose as writers. That is why we exist.

In 2007 Jalal Barzanji became Edmonton's first PEN Canada Writer in Exile, and devoted the year to writing his memoir, and working with writers in the community. The Kurdish poet had been imprisoned from 1986 to 1989 because of his writing. In Iraq, Barzanji edited several magazines and worked at many cultural organizations. He has published six collections of poetry and fiction: *Dance of the evening snow*, *Unwarm*, *War*, *Holy Rain*, *Memory of a Person under the Wind*, and *On Going Back to my Birthplace*. Barzanji served on the board of the Iraqi Kurdish Writers Union, and was executive director of the Culture Department in the Kurdish autonomous region of northern Iraq.

Arriving in Alberta in 1998, Barzanji studied English at NorQuest College and subsequently worked with the Edmonton Mennonite Centre for Newcomers and the Multicultural Health Brokers Cooperative. In 2000 he organized the Canadian Kurdish Friendship Association and won the RISE Award for his work with newcomers. He lives with his wife Sabah Tahir and their children in Edmonton.

RITA ESPESCHIT
Kaleidoscope

SHABNAM SUKHDEV

Some stories are born submissive to prose. They lie flat on the writer's operating table, their will surrendered to the writer's scalpel. A precise cut, and the surgeon writer opens the story's belly, whole paragraphs gently exposed, layer after layer of what happened, how, when and why. There are stories like that, and there is the story that brought me here.

We have wrestled furiously, my story and me. Finally, I managed to cut it open—only to see it explode before my eyes, spreading around a shifting kaleidoscope of floating memory fragments. No recognizable beginning, climax, or end. No comforting sequence to follow.

I decided to pick up random pieces among all those flying plot fragments. Like this one I've just caught now: a yellow piece of memory, coming down like a falling leaf, smelling of moisture and grass. I unwrap it from its tinfoil cover and find inside a fresh memory of our first Canadian autumn. It's cold, and I'm a parent volunteer on a school field trip. My daughter's class is visiting a marsh or a bog or whatever name that specific kind of wetland has in English. Alice is a ten-year-old girl on planet Earth, but she's only a half-year-old baby on planet Canada. She looks at the still waters in the bog and says, "Something's not right." Born in Brazil, my tropical daughter bends down to touch it, and her face brightens up like a flashlight. "Ice!" she screams. The other kids look puzzled. Alice talks to a kid: "Look, so-and-so, it's ICE!" Jane Doe or Joe Doe, can't remember which, looks at the water and answers, very matter-of-factly: "So?" And there's this magical moment, this collision-of-universes moment, when two aliens stare at the same object and each sees a completely different picture.

The fragment wraps itself back and escapes my hand. Now I pick up a light memory that got entangled in my eyelashes.

We are visiting Brazilian friends in Edmonton, a year before we moved here. My friend and I stand beside a marked crosswalk, and I tell him I'm not convinced a car will actually stop for us. My friend laughs. "You know what my mother did when she first came to visit?" he asks. He tells me how she would head to the crosswalk and have a good time playing at the Civilized Driver Amusement Park. It worked like this: when a car came into sight, she'd get closer to the curb—close enough that a car stopped for her. With the car fully stopped, she would move away, without ever crossing the street, so the (enraged, I presume) driver could resume his or her driving. My friend's mother then waited for another car and did it all over again. That poor little old lady. I guess the magnitude of this new-found pedestrian power—something we lack on Brazilian streets—was too much for her. She had to use it and re-use it, until it was assimilated into her cells and life could go on as before.

The memory giggles, it flies away, and I quickly grab another. I know it's a fairly new memory, although it has no date tag.

I am filling out a form and get stuck on a question. "Are you a member of a visible minority?" the form asks. How am I supposed to know? I mean, there aren't many options available here. I have to be either Asian, Hispanic, black, or aboriginal. Hispanic won't do: Brazil was never colonized by Spain, and my broken Spanish wouldn't qualify for the required language identity. I'm not even a *visible* minority, at least not here. I used to be, in Brazil, where my milky skin granted me kind nicknames like "peeled cockroach" and others. The thing is, the form is missing a category: the category of "*audible* minority." Sure, if I'm mute and quiet, most people won't take me for an immigrant. But I say a single word, and up they go, the xenophobic antennae. The antennae wag and scout until they find out I come from the wrong side of the equator line, and—*thump!*—the stamp comes down, a "minority" label printed on my forehead in bright red ink, same colour as the stamper's neck.

Another memory disappears. The next comes wrapped in green and yellow, the colours of the Brazilian flag.

I am behind the wheel of my old Beetle in Belo Horizonte, the city of three million people where I used to live. It's a hot afternoon, so hot that I risk stopping at a red traffic light with my window open. Bad, bad idea. Out of nowhere comes this nine- or ten-year-old boy. He holds a knife to my neck and demands money in exchange for my skin integrity. "Twenty bucks, or I'll slash your throat," he threatens. I have no money on me, which is an idea even worse than the open window. Sitting on the passenger seat, there's a memory game featuring soccer players. I always keep toys in the car for the little kids who ask for money. The boy with the knife isn't really asking. He's way past the little-kid phase, he's visibly high, but I risk a move anyway: "I have no money, but I've got this memory game here. Do you know how to play?" He hesitates for a few bizarre seconds, a boy wondering whether he should stab someone or learn to play a game. "No," he finally answers. "I don't. How do you play?" I teach him, and he's soon joined by a friend who has just finished robbing the other car. They sit on the sidewalk and start playing as I drive away.

The boys float and fade away in the kaleidoscope of my room. I spot another memory, right beside my bed.

We have just moved here, and we want to go out for dinner, but have no idea where. My husband and I browse the Internet, and we notice something that might help us to choose a restaurant: a good number of them seem to have been inspected by some sort of sanitary authority. It's probably safer to eat at those. At least that's what we're able to conclude reading the phrase *fully licensed*. Although we wonder: Why would anyone want to eat in a restaurant that hasn't been licensed at all?

Another plot piece lands on my hand. It is a repetitive plot, played by different characters who recite the same line. "You're so brave," they say. "I'd never have the courage to leave everything behind like you did." There is always admiration in their voices when they say it, and I can't help but feel like a fake.

Brave? Me? True, I quit a good job as the editor at a publishing house. My husband quit a senior management position in the IT sector. We sold everything and moved to Canada. We had no idea whether we would find new jobs in Alberta, and we'll probably never be able to retire. But still, they're all braver than us—the ones who stayed. Some stayed because they had no choice, no money; others because they are heroes, and they are there fighting every day for a better country, for a better future.

Not us. We panicked. We saw our neighbour tortured for his bank PIN through a terrible night; we saw another neighbour's daughter kidnapped for ransom; we saw the bullet hole on my sister's bedroom window. We saw this and so, so much more, and we panicked. We left. We were cowards, not brave.

This memory takes longer to reach orbit—it's a little heavier, it requires more momentum. Once it finds its place, the fragment moves gracefully and effortlessly like the others. Then I see: it's not chaos, the force behind all these facts, voices, and faces that emerge and submerge in the uneasy ocean of my memory. It's another kind of order. I still can't master its logic, but I know it's there. I look again at the kaleidoscope: I don't see order, but I see beauty. It is my story. It is everyone's story. And stories, like the people who are owned by them, they are all that matter.

Rita Espeschit was recently appointed Edmonton's PEN Canada Writer in Exile for 2008–2009. She is the author of thirteen published books of children's literature, two poetry collections, two staged plays, and two screenplays. She is also the co-author of a series of eight language arts textbooks for Brazilian children. As a journalist, Rita has worked for leading Brazilian newspapers, magazines, and TV stations. She has received numerous literary awards and national prizes, including the prestigious Jabuti National Prize. After moving from Brazil to Alberta in 2001 with her husband, Mario Flecha, and daughter, Alice, she continued to write for a Brazilian audience in Portuguese as she began to write in English for publication in Canada. Her play for children, *They're Not Like You and Me*, was produced at the Sprouts New Play Festival in 2008.

MOHAMMED AL-NASSAR
Waiting

TRANSLATED FROM ARABIC BY SOHEIL NAJM
POETIC EDITING IN ENGLISH BY SUSAN BRIGHT

Talking led me to the graveyard.
Talking with my friend,
who was speechless,
led me to the graveyard.

I could not return the ring to the sand.
It jumped from my brother's finger
at a washhouse for the dead.

I saw my country raving.
The river—I saw it
as a black knife.

Oh friend!
Oh neighbour!
Oh desert!

I was obliterated
by your stony rain, my eyes effaced,
my flight, obsessed and desolate,
unable to reach my country,
unable to reach exile.

Oh speechless friend
across a fallen fence!

≈

I found a pigeon
that neither cried nor wailed.

Around it were drawings
of children without limbs
and I remembered,
Oh friend!
the ring
that slipped
from my brother's finger
and fell into the water.

Can we then find,
Oh friends, Oh neighbours!
the ones who were lost
in the graveyard itself lost
beneath another graveyard
that was red?

What you say is wrong
my friend, my neighbour!

The moon didn't fall.
The limb of the space
was broken.

What you say is wrong.

This is not a crazy time
it is the Street,
long and desolate.
What you say is wrong.

This is not an injured sun,
it is the only sun
of a forlorn house.

People have left it,
gone away.

Oh friend, oh neighbour, desert!
nothing remains but winter buried
under a heap of firewood
and I almost smell the odour of fresh dead
rise up with this sandstorm,
that put out the lamp you left over there.

≈

Oh neighbour!
Oh Friends!

This is the black house.
These are its ghost inhabitants
and those are the banners,
like bleeding snow.

And when
arrows clash

everywhere,
when
the emperor
prepares another feast
for our foggy country,
I will remember
rolling my eyes
over the washhouse
and the lies that swallow war.

I will arrange
chess pawns
on the table,
desperate,
but not dead
because
I can
move my teeth
and with my fist I can catch
the beasts of the wind
opening the door with this hand,
which the bird and the bough mock,
and when
the nightmare brings me back
to the "execution field,"
I will jump fully terrified
and scratch at the chest
of the poor light.

Oh friend, Oh neighbour!
I will inspect your forlorn window
and your tree that gives us figs
at the end of summer,
and with the fullness of my despair,
I will breathe this strange fresh sleek air like a memory
empty from the sense of dawn
full of dumb desire,

and I will surrender to sleep
because I will be a morsel to the animal of hope no longer.

As for life,
Oh friend, Oh neighbour, desert!
as for this excellent cage
for taming sparrows and children,
as for the burning tears
my country weaned me on,
I swim in a sanctuary of ash
and go on
like wind,
rain,
or idols
putting
my ear on the track of that railway
that goes to the graveyard,
because I can do only one thing
in these ravaged times:

Continue
to wait for a miracle
to return my ring of shock,
and my country, to me
so I can awaken from
this life.

Born in Iraq in 1961, Mohammed AL-Nassar received a BA in English literature at the University of Baghdad in 1987. He has published poetry, articles, essays, and reviews in many Iraqi magazines in the past twenty years. He was a professional journalist for more than fifteen years in Iraq and in Jordan, where he lived for four years before he came to Canada in 1998. He has published three collections of poetry: *Normal Days* (Baghdad, 1992), *Competition in the Desert* (Baghdad, 1993), and *Third Life* (Beirut, Lebanon, 1996). His writing has also appeared in five anthologies. The poet lives and works in Edmonton. He dedicates "Waiting" to the people of Iraq.

THUC CONG
Revolving Doors

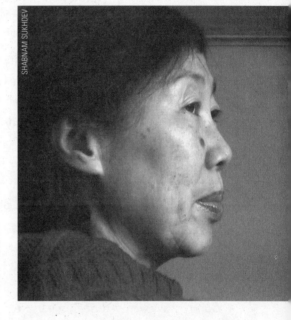

SHABNAM SUKHDEV

I am a devoted Buddhist. Buddhists always talk about revolving, or to be precise, *samara*. Life revolves. Birth revolves. Joy revolves. Sorrow revolves. Anything that exists will revolve and there is a continuation between existence and revolution.

The biggest revolution of my life came too suddenly. It started minutes after I left the Tan Son Nhut Airport and landed at the Thai International Airport. After a few hours waiting for my paperwork, I was on a flight carrying me to Canada via Hong Kong. Within hours I had travelled through two other countries.

My group and I had to stay in a hotel in Hong Kong for the night. Nobody could sleep because we were all worried about our future. We were not sure if the trip would be a smooth one or if there would be any problems. The fear of being detained by the Communists back home still haunted us.

We passed the night in a foreign hotel room with fear and anxiety.

From the darkness came sighs, dry coughs, and soft prayers. Six o'clock in the morning arrived at last. We followed the guide to a restaurant for breakfast. I was very hungry because I had not eaten anything since I left my country. I was too afraid to order some food. I was worried that I could not afford to pay. I looked at the plates of dumplings, rice rolls, and *shiu mai* on the table next to me and tried to swallow my saliva. I secretly reached into my pocket, feeling the twenty US dollars, and told myself I should not spend it. That's all I had. My journey was far from complete so I had to save my money for an emergency. Later on, when I told this story to my husband, he laughed. He told me that everything had been included in the airfare.

The Jet Boeing 747 landed at the Edmonton International Airport on a calm evening in September 1985. I felt so safe now. I had finally come to a free country. At the same time, I felt a vague sense of guilt. I had come to Canada in a safe way while hundreds of thousands of Vietnamese people had risked their lives for freedom. They boarded small boats, ill-equipped, launched to the wild sea, hoping to find freedom somewhere else. Some made it; some did not. It was not fair for the perished ones, but there was nothing I could do about that. The Buddhist in me explained it was their karma. I prayed for the ones who died during their search for freedom.

I came a long way to meet my husband, Sonny, who had escaped Vietnam three years before. I will tell his story now.

Sonny was twenty-nine, a science teacher, when he quietly left the country during the Lunar Year Festival. It was hard for him to leave his family, and me, behind on a special occasion like this. However it was a perfect time to leave as the police were busy celebrating the New Year, and the border would not be under tight guard. Sonny had to grab his chance. We bid each other goodbye on a dark night and hoped we would reunite soon. Neither of us could have imagined that it would be three years until we saw one another again.

His escape was not easy. After leaving Ba Ria, Vung Tau, the boat had some problems. At first, the engine was not working. Without wasting any time, Sonny used his scientific mind to identify the problem and fix it. Then, the boat hit a rock resulting in a severe leak at the bottom. The desperate escapees tried to empty the water and use whatever they could to fill the hole. After that they ran out of food and the most important living element, water. The captain became severely seasick and could not control the boat. Without any knowledge of navigation, but with the strong will to survive, Sonny grabbed the steering wheel. He managed to survive the open sea and brought fourteen other people safely to Malaysia where he stayed in Pulau Bidong refugee camp for two months. Later, he came to Edmonton under the sponsorship of a church. Safely landed in a free country, the boat person still carried in his head a sad memory of the name Pulau Bidong.

Pulau Bidong was an island that belonged to Kuala Terengganu, a state in Malaysia located about 500 kilometres northeast of Kuala Lumpur surrounded by the South China Sea. Between 1975 and the late 1990s about half a million boat people stayed at Bidong and another famous refugee camp called Galang, an island in Indonesia. Those half a million boat people were the lucky ones. An estimated 800,000 people perished in the sea or were killed by the pirates. Women were cruelly and repeatedly raped by the pirates while their fathers, spouses, or boyfriends were killed for trying to protect them.

In 2005 the overseas Vietnamese communities built a memorial to the refugees in Pulau Bidong. The Communist government of Vietnam put pressure on the Malaysian government to demolish it in June of the same year. The front of the memorial read:

> In commemoration of the hundreds of thousands of Vietnamese people who perished on the way to freedom (1975–1996). Though they died of hunger or thirst, of being raped, of exhaustion or of any other cause, we pray that they may now enjoy lasting peace.

The back of the memorial at Pulau Bidong read:

> In appreciation of the efforts of the UNHCR, the Red Cross and Malaysian Red Crescent Society and other world relief organizations, the Malaysian Government and people as well as all countries of first asylum and resettlement. We also express our gratitude to the thousands of individuals who worked hard in helping the Vietnamese refugees.

Although the memorial has been demolished, the Vietnamese boat people still carry the image of it in their hearts. It honoured the traumatic journey that many refugees like Sonny had experienced.

My own journey was so much easier. The Edmonton International Airport impressed me right in the beginning. The new land mesmerized me with its well-lit airport and its gorgeous appearance. Even nature here looked completely different. The air smelled different. It seemed there was more oxygen in the air, and with every breath I took, I noticed a different aroma. Was it the flowers? Was it the people? Was it the freedom? The sky looked different, too. It seemed bluer and higher. Alberta seemed wide open and inviting. Could the air and sky be symbols of my freedom?

I was also impressed by the revolving doors at the Edmonton International Airport. It was the first time I saw an unusual door like that. The exit had several doors—later I learned its technical names, wings or leaves—moving around a centre shaft. The diameter was large enough to accommodate strollers or luggage. The glass doors allowed people to see when a person was coming in or getting out so that collisions would not happen. The doors were also designed for one-way traffic so that people would enter in the right direction. The beauty of a revolving door was that it was always closed and always open; it also permitted free-flowing traffic, allowing the users to enter or exit easily.

For some odd reason, I knew that first day that my life would be revolving like these doors. Once I stepped into the system I had to keep moving, no stopping in the middle of the process. I was entering a completely new society, a new culture. My former life in Vietnam had to recede to make room for a new life in Canada. I had left my country for a country that I thought would give me more freedom and lots of opportunities. The future held the truth.

For the moment, the only truth I knew was that I had lost everything to uncertainty. I was confused about the myths and facts of Canada, but the excited woman inside me could not really tell the difference. As I started my new life, I knew some doors would open for me and some would stay shut. I had to be confident enough to walk through the open ones and strong enough to confront the closed ones.

While I was so lonely and homesick, Christmas came. It was the first time in my life I experienced a real Christmas with real snow.

People around me showed their excitement about the season. Family members gathered to celebrate; relatives and friends exchanged Christmas cards and Christmas wishes. I heard Christmas music everywhere. Everybody baked. Everybody put up Christmas trees. The children were the happiest people, and their smiling faces reminded me of the most important festival in our country, Tet, the lunar New Year.

I remembered Vietnamese children, in their new clothes, folding their arms in front of their parents and grandparents waiting for the lucky money in the red envelopes. Other images surfaced. I smelled the odour of fresh paint from the house after my brothers applied the final coat before the holiday. I could smell the preserved fruits my mother made: limes, mangoes, ginger roots, lotus seed, in the form of candies. My mom cut out small pieces of colourful paper and fringed both ends of each piece. Then she placed the candy in the centre and twisted both ends. Now the candies were well wrapped and the fringes made them look like flowers. My sisters and I helped Mom wrap these candies and place them in a decorated tin. Visitors would be treated to these goodies. Once in a while we asked Mom if we could eat some "ugly" pieces. Our mother's sweet smile was her reply. Yes, it said.

I heard the same Christmas saying everywhere in Edmonton. *I'm going home for Christmas.* It just made me cry. They were going home. Why couldn't I? Did I even have a home to return to? The home on the other side of the globe that I had once owned I had traded to the Communist government in exchange for the exit visa. I might not have an opportunity to go back.

Even when I had been settled in the heart of Edmonton for six years, I still didn't believe that I was far away from my family and my homeland. I thought about Saigon, a huge city of more than six million people, the capital of Vietnam. Living in Saigon had been tough, not only because of high living costs, but also because of the lifestyle. There were more needs, more expectations, and heavy competition.

Yet living here in Edmonton was even tougher than living in Saigon, especially for a woman like me with big dreams in her heart. Dreams might or might not come true. It depended on how well I would adapt, culturally and mentally, to the big change in my life. *Where was my home?* This was the question I always considered. Was it where my soul should be or where my physical body should be?

After six years struggling with nostalgia, stress, school, and odd jobs, I realized some of my dreams. As a former language teacher, I had hoped for a career in an educational institution. My dream of being a teacher again somehow came true although I did not teach directly. Working in a library at a college, I helped students with their research and tried to make their studying a lot easier. My job gave me the opportunity to meet students and teachers who taught me a lot. Every day I learned something new and encountered a new face. Every day I appreciated my job even more. I wished I had come to Canada sooner. There was so much to learn, so much to do, and so much to enjoy. I regretted all the activities and opportunities that I had missed. I had to catch up with the lost years. I had to race with the clock, taking any chance to live my life to the fullest.

My smaller dream was to write the stories of my life in English. Somehow that dream was able to sneak into my busy schedule. On a quiet morning at work, I took a moment to look out of the window. My colleagues had said that my office was "a room with a view." I had been too busy to notice the view until now.

Unlike Vietnam, Canada has four seasons with obvious changes. Winter in Alberta is cold and white. Spring is cool and cheerful with green buds and flowers. Summer, the shortest season, is full of sunshine and rain, sometimes. Now, the country was in its loveliest season of the year—fall.

From my office on the fourth floor of a brick building, I could see the gorgeous painting of nature with its bright yellow of wild flowers, green leaves on a red-brown background of dying leaves. Down below, I could see the North Saskatchewan River. While I was daydreaming, my phone rang, bringing me back to Earth.

It was an editor at the *Edmonton Journal* telling me she would run my article in the next day's paper. I was thrilled. I had published stories in Vietnamese, but this was the first time I had something published in a Canadian newspaper. I had written this commentary for fun with a humble hope that I could share my difficulties, and my experiences, with new immigrants to Canada. Magically, the article turned me from an ordinary person into a hero.

My phone rang non-stop after the article appeared in the newspaper. For me, the honour came in the calls of immigrants from different ethnic groups and from some ESL teachers in the city. The coordinator at the New Home Centre invited me to give a speech to her students on their graduation day that week. My life revolved another time! It was hard to believe that in just a day I had become a guest speaker. I hoped my speech would inspire the newcomers and help them open the closed doors that blocked their way to a better future.

I am still amazed by the door systems in Western countries. Some have a built-in sensor that open the door as you approach it. Some doors slide open; some open when you press a button. Some need to be pushed or pulled. Some you have to pry open. Some stay locked. Of all these systems, I appreciate the revolving door most because it is built on Buddhist theory.

Sometimes Canada is called the revolving door for immigrants. I think of it in another way. Today, as I walk through the revolving door in a downtown office tower, I remember the airport door I passed through twenty-two years ago. I think of Buddhist teaching again. The door stops at a point, then restarts and stops, like life ends and starts over in the life cycle. Change is basic to our lives, and change is what Buddhism is all about. In Pali, the language that the Buddha spoke when he was alive, this change is called *Anicca*. It occurs every second but we do not notice. As Buddhist writer, Thanissaro Bikkhu, writes in *All About Change*:

> Insight into change teaches us to embrace our experiences without clinging to them—to get the most out of them in the present moment by fully appreciating their intensity, in full knowledge that we will soon have to let them go to embrace whatever comes next.
>
> Insight into change teaches us hope. Because change is built into the nature of things, nothing is inherently fixed, not even our own identity. No matter how bad the situation,

anything is possible. We can do whatever we want to do, create whatever world we want to live in, and become whatever we want to be.

Change cannot be avoided. If we understand this, we will manage our birth or death, joy or sorrow, success or failure, satisfaction or disappointment. Having learned a lot from the Buddha's teaching, I apply the term *Anicca* to every change in my life. I always choose the revolving door if I have a chance. It is amazing to step into a space that fills me with a joyful sense of revolution!

Thuc Cong is a prolific writer in the Vietnamese language and in English. Since she arrived in Edmonton in 1985, she has published three collections of poetry in Vietnamese, *A Break in the Cloud*, *Dance on the Horizon*, and *Dawn's First Light*. She has also published five collections of stories in Vietnamese under her pen name Hoang Du Thuy. Thuc earned an education degree at the University of Saigon and was a high-school teacher there before she moved to Canada. Here in Edmonton she has published freelance columns in the *Edmonton Journal*. In 2008 she began working on first book in English, *Through an Immigrant's Pen*.

ATHIANN MAKUACH GARANG

War Tore Us Apart

That early morning, at around 3 AM, I can still remember as clear as the crimson edge of a sunrise. It was a cold, windy, cloudless morning; the moon shining made the night like day. Cocks crowing, dogs barking, cats mewing, the cattle mooing, sheep and goats bleating. They knew that war had come.

My country Sudan is a prosperous country, but its people have had no chance to enjoy comfort or peace. Development is only found in the northern part of the country while there is nothing in southern Sudan. No good roads, hospitals, or schools.

The war came to us one morning. My uncle and cousins and I left our beloved Sudan like storm-driven birds, going into the nowhere.

The trees were waving; I guessed they were saying goodbye to us. It was very hard for a child like me—only six or seven—to leave his mother and siblings behind. War tore us apart. Now the daylight was almost breaking. The birds were singing. Maybe the birds, too, knew that I was leaving them and wanted to say goodbye. I could hear gunshots; we had small hope for survival. From fear, my body quivered like jelly. Overwhelmed, I ran liked a gush of wind that blows across the grass.

Tumult was everywhere. The trees were not happy because they, too, knew that the war had started; it was the beginning of horror and destruction. The effect of the powerful artillery and missiles was like blades slicing the earth. Black smoke filled the air. That day, the day the Arabs of northern Sudan attacked our village, I witnessed the death of my uncle. He was killed. I had lost my own father before I was born; this uncle had been like a father. The Arabs killed him like it was nothing. These are people who are filled with prejudice against us, down deep to their bones; they are on a mission to wipe us from our country, Sudan. They came to towns and villages killing men and abducting women and children, later to use them as slaves in their homes in Khartoum. Young girls and women were raped and killed if they did not comply with the Arabs' demands. Once, when the strangers attacked, I ran with my mother and brothers into the bush. This time, though, the attack was from the bush, home and town, and we were separated. My mother was gone. I was only a small child, and I didn't know what happened to her.

Somehow I escaped unharmed with another uncle, Athiann Deng Garang, my cousins and my kinsmen. Now we walked. Through the forest, day by day, we walked. The highways connecting cities and towns were death traps: full of ambushes and scattered with landmines. The landmines were meant to kill us. The Arab militants didn't want us to live like them. They think they are the only human beings, that we are not even human.

With my uncle and cousins, I walked up and down the valleys and the rivers hoping to find safety. My smooth feet cracked and filled with thorns. Each step I took was labour. My feet were swollen, bruised; I complained, but who could I complain to? We had to keep walking.

We journeyed by night so that we could avoid being seen and also to avoid the hot sun. The sun was hot enough that it could bake an insect that mistakenly tried to cross the road. Sometimes during our night walks

I would hit a tree when sleep overtook me. The stones and the trees were stained with blood; blood was everywhere. When an enemy plane spotted us, the bullets would fall like rain and we would disperse into the bushes. Later we would emerge and find ourselves again.

My feet could not carry me any longer, but still we continued. Our souls needed peace and safety. We would journey from morning to around noon then take a rest under the trees in the forest. We rationed the little food that we had, and there was not enough water for everybody, if there was any at all. Sometimes I cried until tears stopped coming. I was thirsty and hungry. I would chew the bark of a succulent plant to use its sap for water.

Then, after two days of walking without water and food, we came to a lake. The water in this lake was muddy and full of bacteria. But it was water, so that did not matter. It provided life and gave us a second chance. I remember thinking that if I could see the sun rise I had a chance to live for another day. On the evening at the lake, my uncle spotted a gazelle wandering among the tall trees. He took its life to save ours.

It was hot and dry, approaching March, one of the hottest months of the year. We left the lake in the afternoon. The sun rays shimmered like they were doing a belly dance. The temperature was more than forty degrees Celcius, too hot for my little feet. Blisters formed. We continued to travel during the night in the forest. Sometimes one of my kinsmen would die, from hunger or thirst, from the war, or in attacks by wild animals.

At times I wanted the earth to open up and swallow me alive so that I could forget the hardships and suffering I was going through. I would even think in my mind that it would have been better if I were not born so as to avoid this disaster. For us, for thousands of southern Sudanese, the trek to Ethiopia was long and only a few would make it.

It took us four months to cross Sudan to Ethiopia. My cousins and my uncle and I came to Ethiopia in 1989. We had lost our dignity, citizenship, and now we were called refugees. They took us to a refugee camp. Life in the refugee camp was horrible: sanitation was poor, there was no food, not enough water, no better place to live. We were asked to make our own living place from poles, mud, and grass. What kind of a house could they expect from young children like me? We were isolated like sick animals quarantined from the rest of the herd. Some people would jeer at us just because we were refugees.

In this camp, my cousins and I were sent to a group of children to become "red soldiers." I came to realize later that we were being trained as child soldiers. It was terrifying. Confused and traumatized, I did not say a word but let my fate take its course. I went to school for the first time in my life. I felt like someone who had lived under the ground and then was exposed to the sunlight for the first time. The sun felt bright as a shooting star.

Though having a chance to go to school was good, I was emotionally detached and drained. We never knew what would happen to us. In 1991, the Ethiopian president Mengistu Haile Mariam was overthrown and we were no longer welcome in Ethiopia. The Pinyidou refugee camp was near the Gillo River and many Sudanese refugees drowned during the attack by the Ethiopian troops as they tried to cross the river back to Sudan. Thousands of Sudanese refugees jumped into the river and never came out again.

We fled back to Sudan; however the war was still going on. So we fled to Kenya, and in 1992 we were put into another refugee camp. The camp was called Lokichokio. In this camp, life was tough. One night, the troops loyal to John Garang came at night to take my uncle away. My uncle managed to keep them from hurting him and us.

The next morning my uncle approached officials with the United Nations High Commissioner for Refugees and voiced his concern that our lived had been threatened. They took us to Kakuma, a town several miles away from Lokichokio where they had their compound and gave us a place to stay. Here, we thought we were safe but instead one of the local officials was secretly arranging for troops to come to take us to Sudan and possibly have my uncle killed. My uncle was educated and understood what was going on. One night he told us we had to leave the compound to run to a town named Lodwar, far away from Kakuma.

We walked through the forest to avoid being spotted by Kenyan authorities and UNHCR officials. We spent three days walking; by the fourth day we were all exhausted, feet swollen and blistered. We were walking by the roadside that morning when a Catholic sister spotted us from her car. She gave us a lift to Lodwar town and reported us to the Kenyan police. The police phoned the UNHCR compound in Kakuma town stating that they had found us. Officials came to talk to us in Lodwar town asking us whether we would like to go back to Kakuma. We all said no. The police were ordered to force us into the truck. They grabbed us by the neck and legs and threw us into the truck like bags of rice. I was only ten! I was injured. My uncle's hands were tied. We did not have a choice. We were tied up and taken away like thieves back to Kakuma.

One day our persistence for survival finally paid off. We were taken to a camp in northeastern Kenya. This camp was called Hagadera and the majority of the refugees in this camp were Somalis. Life in the camp was hard. It was hot and dry, like a bowl of dust, with temperatures in the mid-40s. We lived in fear knowing that we could die at any moment. We were discriminated against and were not allowed to mix with other children. There were bandits everywhere, armed to kill and take away the few belongings we had. And our souls! The terror and horror, fear and tears. Hide and seek is the game we played at night, but it was serious. We really were hiding, and they really did want to find us.

I was introduced into different cultures and societies at Hagadera. The separation between races broadened, and in the camp I was treated like an outsider. I did not belong anywhere. I was called derogatory names at school. When I touched a water tap it was washed with disinfectant several times before any one else used it. I still remember one time in Hagadera when we had to go for three days without food. My eyes become dark. Under these conditions I went to refugee school and when I came back to our cottage there would be no water and food. This would force me sometimes to go and fetch water, which could take a whole day of standing in the hot sun. But for food I had to wait until UNHCR would find something from sponsors and well-wishers. I spent eight years at Hagadera.

After spending many years in East Africa, frustrated, desperate, and traumatized, my cousins and uncle and I were granted asylum to come to Canada. I arrived in Edmonton with my uncle and cousins on April 8, 2004. Here in Canada, life is tough, but at least I have found a place I can call home, where there is some peace. I plan to finish school and find a way to serve my new community, and my people back in Sudan.

Athiann Makuach Garang is an Edmonton poet whose work has been published in *Legacy* magazine. Born in the village of Abouk, in southern Sudan, he fled the civil war with his uncle, Athiann Deng Garang, and the cousins mentioned in this story. Earlier in the civil war in Sudan, the poet's father, Makuach Garang Yak, was severely injured in an attack. "He came home to us, unconscious on horseback, and we lost him seven days later," Garang says. After many years in refugee camps in East Africa, he arrived in Edmonton in 2004. He graduated from NorQuest College and is now studying at Grant MacEwan College in the university transfer program. While he was reunited with his mother, Ajont Malueath Deng, in a telephone call, he has not yet been able to visit her in southern Sudan. He hopes to publish a collection of his poetry in Canada.

PATRICIA LÓPEZ DE VLOOTHUIS
Call Me Taco, Taco John

I inhale Canada and exhale Mexico. I sweat in English and in Spanish and my teardrops fall in French. I start my jokes in one language and hit the punch line in another. I am a citizen of two worlds, the earth daughter of two nations, the product and consequence of a mixed upbringing. I am a writer; books are my allies and my pen is my weapon.

My life began as most do, as a product of genealogy and monetary might, influenced by religion, topography, chance, and circumstance. I come from a country many people think they know plenty about and even more have visited inattentively. A land of misunderstood mysticism and unquestionable beauty, a nation for centuries vanquished and ransacked from its roots by First World countries—crooks with fancy government titles—and the local influential men who happen to be their friends.

My mother was born in Amecameca, a picturesque town in Central Mexico between the Popocatépetl volcano and the Ixtaccihuatl mountain, the most recognizable, romantic, and mystery-wrapped natural landmarks in my country. Ixtaccihuatl, the Aztec Sleeping Woman who died of a broken heart when her lover went to war, and Popocatépetl, the brave warrior who upon return, overwhelmed by the news of her death, awaited his own demise mourning by her side. You can't be more Mexican than that.

My father was born in the State of Chihuahua, the largest, richest, and northernmost state in Mexico. Santo Domingo was a small mining town under the shroud of foreign interest, once a cornucopia, now a ghost town on the trail to the Copper Canyon, one of the most beautiful spectacles of nature that God placed in my country. My parents come from places of majestic beauty and geographical grandeur.

I'm a city girl, a *Chilanga*—a derogatory word used by all other compatriots of mine, not born in Mexico City, to describe those of us who make the capital our home. It is a disparaging term, of course, since the rest of the country believes that in the city, all people are wealthy procrastinators who earn their keep effortlessly. Mexico's economic growth relies strongly on its oil fields, agricultural power, and the people who work both—not on employees working in the skyscrapers of the beautiful capital city, or so it is said. My cousins in the countryside talked about me as if I were not in the same room, telling their friends: *Es Patty, mi prima la chilanga.* You couldn't be more Mexican than that.

I was born to a symbiotic twosome who had been married for almost twenty years. Now, in their late forties, they expected me to take my first breath in this world with a number of achievements under my belt. There was no time to waste on kiddie stuff. My parents ran a tight ship and time was an issue. I had to grow up fast, before they got too old to outrun me. Their demands for respect involved batting a cane incessantly in the air.

I was molded to be an extraordinarily strange child as every "only child" must be. I jumped higher. I spoke louder. I tried the hardest and the longest. I had to be all that was expected of me in the shortest time, with the least effort.

As a child, I was mesmerized by the anecdotes of the women in my family who had attended boarding schools. I often wondered if it would ever be my turn. I studied in the finest schools in Mexico. When I was eleven years of age, my parents decided it was time for me to leave the cradle and, with uncanny resilience, conquer a foreign learning institution.

Canada was mentioned repeatedly. It was a favourite over France and England. To all of this adult conversation, I paid little attention. French, I could learn, but going to France? Hmm, I would fall behind in my studies if I needed to depend on speaking it fluently from the start. I remember finding solace in the fact that one of Canada's official languages was English, and I was really good at it. Canada sounded like a good idea; at least it was on the same continent. I am sure that my journey here was the result of more extensive thought than just a flip of a coin. I remember my mother reading many books about Canada and visiting the Canadian embassy several times, but what did I know? I was just a child.

My childhood knowledge of Canada was biased, superficial, and limited. Just as anyone's knowledge of any foreign country. Someone, sometime, had pointed out that there were many bodies of water in Canada, and I was afraid of sharks. I wondered briefly if my encounters with sharks could be avoided. I had no say in this decision to leave Mexico. I assumed it was the expected fate of all obedient affluent girls to go away to school. I had a privileged life. I obeyed. And off I went.

At home, I had my own bedroom; a live-in maid washed and cleaned my belongings day after day; all decisions were made for me; and my days were planned. At boarding school in Canada I shared a dorm with nearly thirty girls. I had many friends and no more loneliness. I no longer solicited my mother's tête-à-tête to hear the voice of another nearby human being. Here, commotion and laughter reigned in the most enchanting chaos. I loved Canada. I merged perfectly well. There were no misconceptions about me, and everyone treated me as an equal. My peers respected me as I did them, and the matrons and teachers were as lenient and as harsh with me as they were with my peers. The only time I had privileged treatment was when Patricia Fallmann, my English teacher, said I looked like a lab mouse who had figured out the way to the food at the end of the maze. She believed I needed to expand my frontiers, so she took me shopping and bought me lunch several times, a real treat.

At school I was responsible for my own cleanliness and if I did not dispose of my own dirty clothes in the designated bin at night, it would remain dirty for days. I learned responsibility. At school, nobody nagged me about doing my homework, censored my writing, or made the most picayune decisions concerning my life. I did not need to make myself look busy, pretending to have a great task at hand. I was truly busy, and every task required my undivided attention. I was important. I was in charge. I grew up, I matured, and I became independent and resilient. I embraced this new lifestyle and made this country mine. I wanted to become a Canadian. I wanted to stand tall and sing "O Canada!"

One rainy afternoon in March, Miss Glide notified me that my autonomy had expired. At fifteen, I was recalled home like a product that manufacturers fear may malfunction if left longer in careless hands. The blueprints for the rest of my life were again drawn without my consent, and I had to rearrange my goals to make my parents proud. I was heartbroken the last night I spent in the school. Everyone had left earlier, and I was the only one who would ride to the airport next morning. As I walked the dorm from end to end, I cried in desolation.

As soon as I settled back home in Mexico, I embarked on the venture of teaching English as a Second Language. This is what former boarding-school girls did in their spare time. I needed formal training, so I went to an institute that offered the instruction I needed. Sometime in April 1975, days before my grandma's flowers bloomed and a few days after my mom's last canary died, I suddenly encountered my future. The institute's director was an Anglo-Saxon, blonde, stallion-like Adonis who triggered an eerie effect on me. I can only describe the experience as jaw dropping.

This is when and where all great movies, all Nobel Prize-winning novels, all Pulitzer Prize stories, secure that *je ne sais quoi* that earns them immortality. Music in the background. Drums roll. This is the moment when *Call me Ishmael* came to light, when *Fifty-three years and nine months and four days, that is how long I have loved you* was born, and *It was the best of times, it was the worst of times* and so many more magical moments in the written form were begotten.

Adonis was Canadian. How could anyone be more perfect? I rushed to announce to my parents that I had met the man with whom I would spend the rest of my life. I was sure that they would agree since they constantly voiced their fear that I would eventually forget English if I did not speak it on a daily basis. Tremble no longer, I reassured them. I will uphold your gift forever. With this Canuck by my side, your investment is secure, and my knowledge of the English language will not go down the drain. If my parents needed a whopper of a reason to bless my marriage, I had just pulled an elephant out of the magician's hat. There was no chance they would be displeased. Now I just had to promise them that I would finish my studies, pursue my career as an interpreter-translator, and continue writing—all of which I did, in Mexico.

Life was good. Thirteen years into our marriage, three children, four dead Kamikaze pet turtles later, and with an array of wonderful stories to tell, my husband and I found ourselves celebrating the most memorable Valentine's Day ever.

Candlelight dinner and gourmet dishes on the table, Joe and I started exploring the possibility that our eldest would go to boarding school in Canada, starting a new tradition in our family. Chunk of veal drenched in gravy and peas on top, followed by a "Hmmmm, this is good!" Sip of wine, bite of Tiramisu, followed by a "Cheers honey!" But why did we have tears in our eyes? We were a mess. We just couldn't come to terms with our son departing from our nest, and then, in three more years, it would be time for the second one to fly. And then, to top off our misery, in ten more years, the smallest one would follow, leaving our home empty, barren, and cheerless. What were we thinking? We could not allow this to happen. We had to reverse this decision and break the spell conjured upon my family generations earlier, by women like myself.

We found a balance between tradition and sanity and decided to deploy the whole family to Canada, the remarkable country that opened its frontiers to those under duress. Our children would have the education I wished for them, and that my parents once struggled to give to me, and all without the terrible ordeal of separating from one another.

Taco John, as my eldest was dubbed by his Canadian peers upon arrival to his new school, embraced the change of country with the most enthusiasm. My son spoke English with a slight accent, which he learned to exploit as time passed. He discovered that Taco preceding his name, far from being a derogatory term, was his passport to the land of beautiful girls. Give him lemons, he makes *Agua de limón*. Johnnathan should have lost his hint of an accent within months; however, by his first year of high school, he was speaking English as heavily as Antonio Banderas, and Katie, the most gorgeous girl in the school, was his girlfriend. When Taco John played the guitar and sang *Caballo Prieto Azabache* with his exaggerated Latin accent, the males would vent air to the faintish females with flattened six-pack cartons. And those lucky *señoritas* who overcame oblivion, but were now hyperventilating, would strike their chest to the beat of "Oh my God, he's so sexy!" Johnnathan embraced the part so fervently that he would even introduce himself in the manner of Agent-007-meets-Hemingway: "Call me John, Taco John."

Taco John. Chilanga. Déjà vu! Some things are the same everywhere. I was experiencing Canada through a completely different scope than I had decades before. Taco John was just the beginning of a long list of misdemeanours that were eventually rationalized and forgiven:

—When I attended the first parent-teacher meeting in my new country, the guidance counsellor at my sons' school was surprised at so many things. First, that my son Kenny was no snotty, dishevelled toddler wrapped in a *rebozo,* dangling barefoot from my back. Instead, beside me walked a perfectly groomed three-year-old carrying a bucket of Lego, dressed in designer overalls and running shoes. Secondly, I was in my *blonde* stage, embracing the Audrey Hepburn look, hair in a smooth chignon and bangs. I wore a classic Chanel two-piece suit, leather high heels with matching purse, my mom's triple string of Mikimoto Pearls, and an imitation Rolex watch. When I was a child, my mother attended parent-teacher conferences dressed in her Sunday best, and so I did the same. The teacher, Mrs. Fox, stood in complete awe as I introduced myself and my son. She first commented on how "fair" Kenny was and said that we did not look Mexican at all. She expressed great relief, and then she emphasized in complete astonishment (repeatedly) that I was nothing like what she expected. She said it was refreshing to be able to have a meeting with an immigrant mother with whom she could have a two-way conversation.

—Father Sylvan, the Catholic priest, greeted us at our new home and offered the assistance of a community volunteer who would help me to figure out the function of the vacuum cleaner and the dynamic duo of washer and dryer. She would also immerse me in the Canadian way of doing things. He emphasized that his church was very traditional and that he would not tolerate any loosey-goosey behaviour on his watch, unlike some of the Mexican priests who engaged and promoted political feats, taking sides with rebels and putting religion to shame. I believe he thought El Salvador was part of Mexico because there has not been a war in my country since the early 1900s, civil or otherwise. I simply wanted to set the record straight. He never spoke to me after that.

—As a Certified Translator Interpreter, I wanted to continue my career in Canada. Unable to find out how to register my name in the court system, I found my way to the offices of Employment Canada. I plucked an application from the rack on the wall. Everyone in the room was holding a paper of some sort in their hands, so I filled in all the information required and lined up to take a number. "When in Rome, do as the Romans do" also applies in Canada. Thirty-six numbers later, I was directed to Mrs. Long Face. She vaguely glanced at my paper, hurriedly tossed it back to me as if she were dealing cards in a Las Vegas casino, and said to the table . . . not to me, she never once looked me in the face . . . "Government jobs are only for citizens. What makes you think you will be hired before a Canadian? You might be considered as the first option, but only after the last Canadian."

I was young and naïve and forgiving. I did nothing. I stood up and slam-dunked the paper into the garbage can as I left, spirit wounded. I went home and cried. A few days later, my destiny shifted. Our own barrister, Mr. Kennedy, offered me an opportunity to freelance for his firm. Thanks to his guidance I received my certification in Canada and worked in the legal system for years. My contribution as an interpreter was of crucial importance to many immigrants who were facing a grim fate. I recall the first day in the Assertiveness and Tolerance Training in the Cultural Interpreting Service, someone had written on the blackboard: "If you ASSUME, you make an ASS of U and ME." So true.

—When Chris, my middle son, a.k.a Mex, got into trouble, which he did many a time in both the Mexican and the Canadian way, the meetings with the teachers would start with a teacher's assertion: "We are not sure what you, Mexicans, are used to allowing in your country, but here in Canada . . . " Oh my! One time a teacher had the audacity to point out the possibility that Chris was "like that" because of my Mexican genetic contribution. There was nothing wrong with Chris. He was a child who would stand up and sing his way towards the garbage can at the front of the classroom and sharpen his pencil seven times a day, or until the pencil vanished in shavings. He danced his way to the bathroom ten times, had to throw garbage another twelve times, and dropped his book another twenty. He just couldn't sit still. The teacher summoned the boy's Canadian-born father to listen to his complaints. A few minutes into the meeting in the school library, Joe was getting up, glancing at book titles, looking out the window, checking the time, browsing through a Louis L'Amour novel. The teacher followed him around the room with his eyes as he swivelled his body, trying, unsuccessfully, to maintain eye contact. When all attempts failed, his jaw dropped. (Joe had the same effect on me when I first met him, remember?) He closed his black book, got up abruptly, and muttered in complete dismay: "Never mind, it's hopeless."

Time passed and life seemed to evolve more swiftly. The Canadian way worked in unison with the Mexican way. Taco John came to terms with his fame and popularity and is now the award-winning executive chef of a bistro. Mex, a.k.a. Christopher, who was legendary for his wit and his elaborate pranks, became a successful businessman. Kenny had suffered from stuttering when his cognition and understanding of the English language surpassed his ability to speak it. After two years of speech therapy and the new fad of turtle talking, he stopped stuttering completely and now, eighteen years later, he will graduate from McMaster University this spring with his beautiful wife Jeny by his side. I have had a successful and fulfilling career and I can say that I am truly happy in my professional life.

What brought me to Canada was the desire to keep my family together, to find an alternate path to our lives, to enrich my children's history with the experiences that shaped my existence and that would come naturally to them. I came here first for the learning experience; it was my parents' decision. I stayed for the love of this land. This is mine. I am here now, in the city that I feel I deserve, Edmonton, the City of Champions, because we are all victors in our own struggles. We have succeeded in surpassing all hurdles placed before us. I am here to stay. This is my city.

And so . . . my grandchildren's lives will begin as most do, as a product of upbringing, idiosyncrasy, genealogy, and monetary might, influenced by topography, chance, and circumstance.

En conclusión, soy mezcla y diversidad. Vengo de la tierra del nopal, del Indio y el agave, de la pitahaya y la charamusca. La tierra donde la raza de bronce, trabaja la plata en Taxco y los Volcanes resguardan lenitivos, el crecimiento de la gran ciudad.

Mi gente sirve tacos, enchiladas y frijoles negros refritos en sus mesas adornadas con deshilados que hacen con gran atino, las indias de las manos hábiles. Se degusta el Mole de Oaxaca, la birria de Jalisco y la Machaca de Sonora, acompañamos estos platillos con agua de horchata, de tamarindo o guanábana.

Mi país está delineado por dos océanos y otro tanto más de mares. Sus playas son de talco y sus aguas de turquesa. Vengo de la tierra que vio nacer a Octavio Paz y aloja a Gabriel García Márquez, ambos Premio Nobel . . . así na' más. México, el pergamino poético y crítico de Sor Juana y el lienzo virgen que Diego y Frida hubieron de desflorar.

Nací un día en que se recreaba la crucifixión de Cristo, en medio de la fiesta más sonada en mi patria, un martes de Semana Santa. Nací en el país de las abundancias naturales y riquezas por explotar, del clima perfecto, y de las mujeres bellas y abnegadas de las trenzas que se extienden para siempre.

El destino me ha traído aquí, al país de los veranos ardientes, los inviernos gélidos, y las primaveras perfectas. La tierra del otoño esplendoroso y la Aurora Boreales. Llegué a Canadá seducida por sus Grandes Lagos, por Niágara—maravilla mundial. Llegué para quedarme y en esta tierra tan rica de tanto, me he de cimentar. Respeto la hoja de maple magenta en el lienzo rojiblanco, respeto el "O Canada" tanto como mi Himno Nacional y el águila sobre el nopal.

Mis hijos son mezcla de dos razas, producto de dos idiosincrasias, influencia de dos geografías y resultado de una educación mixta. No hay riqueza más grande ni más acertada que la parida de lo mejor de dos naciones, del producto selectivo de la fusión del indio y el sajón.

Soy Mexicana y Canadiense y ciudadana de esta inmersión. Hablo Inglés con ligero acento y español a la perfección. Mezclo vocablos de ambos idiomas en mi conversación, lo cual desde años, ha enriquecido mi comunicación. Lo mismo me tomo una limonada, que un root beer, un tequila añejo reposado, o una Molson bien helada. Empiezo a contar un chiste en Inglés, y lo termino en Español. De México me traigo el café de Chiapas, el axiote de Mérida y las pantimedias baratas del Mercado de Coyoacán; De aquí me llevo el licorice, el condimento Montreal Steak y el café de Tim Hortons. Disfruto los productos y degusto los frutos de lo mejor de dos mundos.

Soy ciudadana de aquí, y ciudadana de allá; Soy mezcla y diversidad.

Patricia López De Vloothuis is a writer and certified translator. After a lifetime of writing for her own pleasure, she submitted a story in a national competition sponsored by a leading newspaper in Mexico City, *Novedades Editores*. Among 200,000 entries, her story won. She entered the competition five times and won three times; the newspaper subsequently published her winning stories in a book. She published her first book, *Eclipse de Mujer*, a collection of twelve profiles of Mexican women, in 1997. She recently completed the second book in the planned trilogy, *Eclipse en el Reino de Nunca Jamás*, which will be published in Mexico soon. She lives in Edmonton with her family.

A.K. RASHID

The Searcher

By 1989, the mujahedin forces in Afghanistan had driven the military forces of the Soviet Union out of the nation. Feuding warlords, trained and supplied by the United States, Saudi Arabia, and Pakistan, then began a violent struggle with one another for control of the country. A third of the population fled Afghanistan as refugees. Powerful warlords fought to dominate the capital, Kabul, terrifying the population in an atmosphere of criminality and chaos.

Kabul was burning; hunger and death ruled the city. The thieves were still, like pests following each other. And the people were still, like animals in front of the butcher's shop, waiting for death under the paws of the killers. They didn't know what would happen to them, in a moment, a day or a night.

For more than three years my family and I suffered from situations that you might not believe. You might consider this an exaggerated story. We faced all of these unbelievable situations . . .

Fifty thousand innocent citizens of Kabul were killed and robbed by those who referred to themselves as freedom fighters, the *mujahedin*. These oppressors had support from the West to fight against the Soviet Union. They destroyed many mosques and brutally burned the holy book of our faith. The city was in such an impossible position that people didn't have enough water for ablutions to pray five times a day to their God, who had created them. Their lovely city was a disaster.

During this time, we went to India, the country that our parents called their second historical home. India gave us shelter, kindness, and peace like a mother would give to her child. Even though we escaped Afghanistan, and were no longer under the rule of thieves or killers, the television news of killing and looting in Kabul shocked us more and more each day.

Within a month or two, we began to hear about the deaths of our relatives or neighbours.

> *Mina, my aunt was shot for not wearing her hijab.*
> *Uncle, Gullo was killed for being a singer.*
> *The school where you studied has been destroyed because it provided education.*
> *A girl named Nahid threw herself from the sixth floor of her apartment before the thieves could assault her.*

We heard news like this each and every day. The thieves continued their looting and killing. At the same time the so-called freedom fighters gave opportunity to smugglers and murderers from other countries to take part in the killing and looting of Afghanistan. They looted and transferred all precious and ancient valuables from our museums, libraries, and archives. We lost thousands of manuscripts, three-thousand-year-old statues, and other important written historical documents.

During the war between the warlords: Masood, Hazara warlords, and Hikmatiar, many innocent men, women, children, and elderly people had to remain in their houses for days, weeks, and months or they would be killed. After that, their relatives would be notified and would come to bury them without any kind of funeral or ceremony because of the war between the warlords and the destroyers of Kabul.

Far away, we were happy in India but we dreamt and thought constantly about our country and our village. We tried to teach our children not to forget their language, culture, and faith, and we succeeded. India was a reasonable place to practice our religion. Historically, India was not a foreign country to us because it was controlled by our ancestral rulers for a long period of time. Our history taught our children not to forget that our people were also once a great power in Asia and were the makers of a strong empire and civilization in this region.

Until 1996 we told our children that the war would soon end, and we would go back to Kabul. However, halfway through that year, one morning after we woke up, my youngest daughter Khaleda turned the television on and heard . . .

> *Kabul is no more under the rule of warlords and killers. It is under Taliban rule.*

We were shocked to hear such news yet many people thought that God had sent the Taliban to kick out the warlords and so called *mujahedin* from our country. In the end they could not form a government that would be accepted by everyone in the country and recognized in the international community. The Taliban came up with their own laws and ideas. After the assassination of the former president, Najibulalh, the intellectual part of Afghan society lost hope and optimism for the future.

Observing this situation my mother quoted a famous saying: "The clothes that the Taliban wear are too long to fit them." She meant that they were not capable of forming a democratic administration because they started their decrees by abusing and insulting human rights, especially the rights of women.

Now the Taliban ruled the nation. They banned music and dancing, shut down movie theatres and television stations, destroyed public works of art that depicted living beings, and banned the consumption of alcoholic beverages. Men were ordered to grow full, untrimmed beards. They were rounded up, beaten with sticks and forced to pray in the mosques five times a day. Women were forced to cover themselves. They were not allowed to be seen outside on the streets without a man who was a near relative.

Afghanistan was in ruins. After the arrival of the Taliban, it was dragged into even more tragedy than before, and lost, in the spirit of a Pashto poem.

yow me la asla rang zeray wa,
bal me janan la yaray wakhistal lasona.
From one side my original colour was yellow,
From the other side, my beloved neglected and left me alone in my love

My children had grown up. For me, the thought of going back to my country was like moving closer to hell. At this point my teaching position in India was about to end, and we had to find a place where our kids could finish their studies. My wife was a professor of history. She knew about the strong multicultural idea that was practiced here in Canada. To her Canada was a country that was similar to India due to this multicultural aspect that existed in both nations. So we decided to apply at the Canadian embassy as immigrants. In a few weeks we received a letter telling us we were eligible. The words stay with me: "We received your letter. Be hopeful in the future."

In 2001 the whole world had to face a new challenge due to the situation in Afghanistan. No one in their wildest dreams could have imagined the destruction of the World Trade Centre in New York the way it happened. We, too, thought that this conflict had no end to it and that moving to Canada was the smartest decision we could make for our future.

America started bombing Afghanistan. They killed a large number of people, and they destroyed the Taliban regime. They said that they would restore peace and democracy to the people of Afghanistan. Unfortunately after a few months, it seemed that the Americans had become friends with the warlords who had taken the lives of thousands of Kabul's citizens just a few years before. The intellectuals of Afghanistan remained the target of the warlords because of the fear that they might question the rules and regulations of the new government, and the chaotic situation the warlords were responsible for creating.

By this time all the educated people had moved out of the country. The new Afghanistan brought with it nothing but drugs, smuggling, and prostitution, which had been forbidden in traditional Afghan society. In the end, anti-government and anti-American sentiments became powerful and finally the result was suicide bombing, which created huge casualties for the peacekeepers and the innocent people of the country.

In March 2002, my wife and I left our jobs as professors in India for three reasons: war in our homeland, injustice in our adopted country, and our hopes for the education of our children. We came to Canada where we gave up all the hot days and nights of Delhi for the cold and snowy scenery of Edmonton.

My family and I are happy about the decision. However, in terms of finding jobs, up until now I have noticed that no place except McDonald's welcomed us. Before I came here I had a feeling that I could spread the knowledge I had accumulated in my life and give it to this lovely country. I was wrong because I have had no opportunity to do so. As far as the future is concerned I do not want to work in such places as fast-food restaurants. I respect my dignity as an intellectual, and I think all of you, dear ladies and gentlemen, will agree with me that it is not reasonable for people like us to let our hard work and our university degrees go in vain. I continue to search for my place here, hoping for something better.

I would like to conclude with a famous saying from my second language, Persian: *molke khuda tang nest . . . paye faqir lang nest.* The world of God is not small; the leg of the searcher is not paralyzed.

A. K. Rashid was born in 1957 in Ghazni, Afghanistan, where he received his early education. He obtained his master's degree from Kabul University in 1979, and later a doctorate, and began a distinguished literary career. His twenty-three published books include three novels, four collections of poetry, four collections of short stories, and many volumes of literary criticism and literary translation. He taught in the faculty of Language and Literature at Kabul University. After leaving Afghanistan for India, he became a visiting professor at the Center of Persian and Central Asian Studies at Jawaharlal Nehru University, New Delhi. He works in Persian, Pashto, English, Urdu, and Hindi. Dr. Rashid and his family arrived in Alberta in 2002 and live in Edmonton.

MONIKA IGALI

Whatever You Do, Don't Ask Me Where I'm From

MARIE SADIVY

When I wondered what it would be like to live in Canada, I never imagined how many times people would ask me the same question.

I might have imagined many different nationalities living together. I might have imagined snow and open spaces, picket fences and huge spruce trees, but never the unending monotony of the first question that most people ask me: Where are you from? I am someone who doesn't want to stand out in a crowd. I don't like to be noticed or to be at the centre of attention. If you're like that, too, I don't recommend immigrating to another country. I'm sure that the question comes from the well-known politeness and healthy curiosity of Canadians, but it gets bothersome to answer them continuously!

It might be interesting to hear how the real Hungarian *gulyas* are made, what language Hungarians speak or if we have answering machines or the Internet in Hungary. You might also want to know how long I've been in Canada, and why I still have such a strong accent. But there is so much more to me and to the country of my birth than all of that. I have views and opinions that have nothing to do with where I am from. I have feelings that can be hurt. I have ideas that resonate with the ideas of others, no matter where they are from. If you really want to get to know me, ask me a new question.

My father travelled all over the world, worked in England and in Canada for a year, and always said that people are the same no matter where you go. I didn't believe him. My mother lived in the same city all her life and always said that people are basically good even though they are different from each other. I didn't believe her either.

Coming to Canada was a dream of mine for a long time, just as it is for so many others still living in Hungary. I get constant questions about what it is like here, and other questions about prices and the weather. I heard one question recently that stuck in my mind: Do people treat you differently when they learn that you are from Hungary? I don't know the answer to that question.

Packing up and moving is not something that is easy to do, and it looked foolish to many that we left Hungary with our two-year-old daughter, two suitcases, and two hundred dollars—for the unknown. I wasn't thinking about the practical part of life, like learning a language, finding a job, and providing food and shelter for our children, and I had never considered the question that continues to follow me wherever I go: Where are you from?

It has been almost twenty years since we immigrated to Canada, yet it only takes a minute—one, unexpected minute—for me to daydream my way back to the streets of Budapest. I can be anywhere, doing almost anything and the next second I am on the December-grey streets of downtown Budapest, looking at the people hurrying about their days, or I am walking on the sloping streets of my neighbourhood where the air is filled with the smell of the flowering linden trees in June.

I grew up there, in the metropolitan atmosphere of a Communist capital with its rich culture and long history. My father loved music and when the first elementary music school opened in Budapest, my fate was sealed. I attended the school for eight years, taking music lessons, singing in a choir, and learning how to play the piano. From an early age, my parents took me to concerts of all sorts: children's, classical, folk, and popular. I went to the theatre with them to see puppet shows, classical productions, and everything in between. The exposure to a stimulating culture made politics invisible to me. When I was young, the injustices and hardships didn't touch me the way they touched my parents, yet the ambience created by my surroundings instilled in me a sense of fairness and the ability to think for myself. At least, that is what I noticed, not when I was growing up, but later, when I was removed from my birthplace to a different environment.

As I got older, politics found its way into my life anyway and my disillusionment heightened in secondary school. Feeling helpless about the political situation, I spent those years with the intention of enjoying my days and looking for kindred spirits. That time gave me a sense of freedom that is still very important to me. I wanted to fit in. I wanted to be understood. I was looking for my ideal, restriction-free life in a society restricted by rules.

I met many people, but only a few provided the safety I was looking for. I met people at the theatre, at sailing camps, at book sales, and at folk dance halls. I spent a lot of time talking and listening to them. Everybody spoke freely, criticized the government or the church without fear of retaliation. That is what I saw. Maybe the government let people vent their frustrations so they would feel that they were not being abused by those in power. Give them the illusion of free speech; that will calm them down!

To me it was normal that parents divorce and one of them gets remarried, the other becomes an alcoholic. It was normal that people smoked and drank. It was normal that every night there would be dozens of places to go to, and dozens of friends to go with. The good and the bad were all mixed into my everyday life. I marched on with all those who wanted something more out of life than simple survival.

Soon after high school, I got married and had a daughter. I stayed home with her in our tiny apartment of thirty-five square metres. In

Hungary, the government provides a three-year maternity leave for mothers who choose to stay home with little ones. When I had my daughter, mothers received 90 per cent of their original salary for the first year and 65 per cent for the two consecutive years. My husband still had to work two jobs: one as a chemical technician, his chosen profession, and another as a taxi driver, for us to make ends meet. After work, he went to work, and than he slept and went to work again.

We left Hungary in 1987, despite restrictions on travelling. We couldn't take much with us because our trip to Austria was supposed to be just a family vacation. We couldn't say good-bye to loved ones properly, because they weren't supposed to know that we weren't coming back in two weeks. We packed two suitcases and went to Austria to apply for refugee status. We spent a few days in a refugee camp near Vienna, sleeping on bunk beds in a huge room in the company of about thirty other families. Later we were transferred to a small town to await the day when we could fly to our final destination: Canada. For seven months, we lived in a *gasthaus*, or bed and breakfast, and than we moved to another small town into another *gasthaus*, but we didn't have time to get comfortable there. After spending only eight months in Austria—a short time compared to the experiences of others—we got the green light to immigrate to Canada.

The airplane left Vienna for Montreal, where we had to spend the night. From there, we flew to Charlo, New Brunswick, and then drove to the small town of Campbellton. I experienced those few days on the road as if I were watching a movie. For somebody as shy as I am, a trip like that is not easy. Instead of hiding away and observing, I had to endure being under the microscope: bombarded by questions from officials and civilians in a foreign environment. I wanted to fit in, like always. The fact that there was another couple from Hungary living in Campbellton didn't make a big difference, because speaking the same language didn't mean that we understood each other. Their personalities, their attitudes, their backgrounds, and their goals were different from ours.

When I look back, I realize that Campbellton was the ideal transitional place for us. In a bilingual community, it wasn't too noticeable that we were different, that we didn't speak the language. Either of them. If we didn't understand what somebody said in English, they assumed that we were French and switched to French. That didn't work, and that's how my husband became known as "the taxi driver who does not speak either English or French." In a store, I witnessed an unusual incident when the cashier could only speak English and the customer could only speak French. Is that bilingual?

I remember how surprised we were watching the news during the first few months. Focusing on what signage should be used—English or French—seemed trivial to us compared to the problems of poverty and political instability that filled the newscasts of Hungary. The question of finding and expressing our identity wasn't important at that stage of our lives. Now I see that in this land of immigrants an identity crisis rears its head even among those who were born here.

In Campbellton we lived in a two-bedroom apartment and got all the help we needed to settle in. My daughter, who had just learned how to speak Hungarian, went to a daycare run by French nuns, where she picked up some French. There was a time when we didn't understand some of what she said. We took an intensive English course for six months. Our teacher tried everything to show us what life in Canada could be. Her approach was enjoyable but not as practical as we needed it to be. If we were students who came over to Canada to learn about life here, this would have been the perfect class to take. She took us on field trips; some of them were more helpful for our future lives than others. Getting a library card had the merit of usefulness, but we also went horseback riding and dug up clams, which are things I haven't done since.

I argued with her over what should be in the curriculum. I felt that expanding my vocabulary was something I could do anytime on my own, but I needed more help to learn grammar. My experience of learning languages was different from her approach. In Hungary, teachers pounded grammar into us continuously. Learning was all work and no play, so going on field trips felt like wasting precious time. Taking a six-week course with the teacher after a disagreement like this could have been unpleasant, but she always behaved professionally, and to this day we keep in touch.

Life went on: daycare, school, work, chores. We were adjusting to Canada, but Campbellton wasn't the place for us. We are from a big city and in that small town there wasn't even a public playground for my daughter. A year after arriving, we packed up and moved to Edmonton, where we had friends we had met back in Austria.

We started all over again in Alberta. I stayed home with our daughter, and my husband got a job as a cab driver. To find a job in his field as a chemical technician, he needed to go back to school, but that would have been a luxury. By then we had two children: in 1990 our son was born. Our life in Canada was not what I had imagined it would be, but it was a good life. It was a life, though, that took all our energy to create. Our family and friends in Hungary asked us about our impressions of the city, and the province, and the country, and politics, and economics. We had no answers for them. We had to focus on our daily lives. We did not go sightseeing until my father came to visit for a few months, and he was the one who took us. That was in 1991 when we had been living here for three years.

It was about that time when I realized that the ideal thing would be to have the best of both worlds: the space and calmness of Canada with the intellectual stimulation and cultural liveliness of Hungary. If only I could have my friends from Hungary and Canada around me at the same time, eliminating the distance of oceans and continents . . . I still wanted to be accepted, to be understood, to be able to fit in. At first, the where-are-you-from questions didn't bother me, because I didn't feel that I belonged yet. But when my son was born here, my daughter went to school here, when I volunteered and worked here, the question didn't make sense anymore.

When my marriage ended in 1998, I had to start all over again. It was inevitable to me that our relationship would have ended, even without the move to a new country, but depending solely on one person—my husband—for everything put more pressure on our relationship. When I was going through my divorce, which was anything but amicable, everyone I talked to asked me the same question: Are you going home? It was everyone's immediate reaction, except mine. Even though I was alone with two kids under the age of thirteen, I instinctively felt that my chances of making it here were better than they would have been back in Hungary where I had family and friends and all kinds of emotional, psychological, and physical support. I still don't know why I stayed; I have never thought about it, but it wasn't a hard choice. It wasn't even an option.

My children feel at home in Canada and in Hungary. We speak Hungarian at home. I taught them how to read and write in Hungarian. On Saturday mornings, they went to the Hungarian school to learn more about the history and literature of their ancestors. They joined the Hungarian Scouts and a folk dance club to become more familiar with our customs and folklore. I thought that the extra knowledge could not hurt, but now I wonder if it contributed to the invisible string that ties them to a place that should be foreign to them.

Going back to Hungary for visits was not without worries either: it was hard to gauge what kind of reactions we would get. There was a time when an emigrant was looked upon, not just with suspicion, but also with resentment. There was another time when having work experiences outside of Hungary became an asset. Questions kept coming from every direction. It was hard to put into words how I felt, or to describe what had really happened. Most of the time I didn't know the answers myself.

From time to time, I still feel like an outsider here. It is impossible to tell if this is because I was born elsewhere, or that I would feel like a stranger back in Hungary, too. Canadians' impressions of Hungary, and of life in a Communist country, are far from what I experienced when I lived there. So what should I do when these topics come up in conversation? It would take so much more time to provide an accurate picture than the attention span of the superficial conversationalist would allow. Aside from the lack of time, people need to hold on to a preconceived picture. They don't want to change it. Change is scary.

The questions keep coming every time I open my mouth. People continue to ask me—you know it by now—where I am from. It doesn't matter what subject is being discussed, the question is there, abruptly, in my face. I know it's not meant to offend me, but how can I fit in, when my accent betrays me? I still get comments almost every day, on what I say, and how I say it. They surprise me so much that I'm lost for words. When I express an opinion about politics, it is always interpreted as being tinged by Communism. Maybe so, but it would be too simple to chalk it up to the first half of my life. It is a ready excuse to invalidate what I say. I think for myself, and I have an opinion, and just because I grew up in a Communist country doesn't mean I am a Communist.

I don't have to be the sentimental type to admit that Canada has given me a lot. I have created a life for myself here. It might not be the life I imagined before I arrived in Canada, but I am able to support my children and myself. We've never been rich, but there was always money for piano and swimming lessons even if we don't go away for holidays. I have a steady job, and I'm able to go to school part time. I don't own a house, but the housing co-operative where we live has given me more than just a roof over my head.

Life in Canada is easier than it would have been in Hungary. There are opportunities here for me and for my two children that would not have been available back home. But do I feel at home? Do I feel like I fit in? Where is home for somebody who has lived her life between two countries on two different continents? And when I'm reminded every day by well-meaning people who make innocent comments that I'm different from the "norm," when I'm still asked every week where I am from—it is hard to feel at home.

What is even more confusing is that even though my daughter was two when we left Hungary and my son was born in Edmonton, both want to go back "home." And how can I fault my children for wanting to go back to Hungary when half of my heart is still there?

I have missed, and will always miss, certain aspects of Hungary: my friends and my family; my favourite candy, *Zizi*; all those bookstores, flower shops, and bakeries that line the streets of Budapest; the theatre productions and concerts. I don't miss other elements: the lack of privacy; the lack of customer service; the lack of money to maintain one of the most beautiful cities in the world. But my father and my mother were right after all. People are the same everywhere and they are basically kind.

In the midst of busy days, I am trying to live up to all the expectations placed on me by society, and by myself. There are so many people who still feel the need to label others, and most of these generalizations are based on stereotypes. For someone who wants to make a new home in Canada, asking the question "Where are you from?" does not help.

Will I ever feel at home in Canada? Perhaps if I stop hearing that question.

Monika Igali was born in Budapest, Hungary, and has been living and working in Edmonton for the past twenty years. She writes poetry and short fiction and is pursuing new opportunities to publish her creative writing. She is completing her final courses in the professional writing program at MacEwan College.

NDUKA OTIONO
Two Poems

Paint the Sky

it's a wet, breezy Friday night
and I will paint the sky tonight
inspired by my wrinkled jacket,
a raincoat that reminds me
of the gossamer feel of condoms.
I'm in an Edmonton bar, alone,
dreaming of homeland and *Maxim*
with all the Stars, pepper soup and
ugba salad that Friday night offers . . .
inside RATT,[1] there're no rats.
the bar is clean like a newly shaved chin
but instead of the fragrance of aftershave
the smell of tobacco hangs in the air

---

[1] Room at the Top, or RATT, a bar at the University of Alberta.

suffocating desire with nicotine
and I, a troubadour, am perched
on a stool with spindly legs like
the stilts of some African
masquerade, facing the window . . .
outside, Edmonton is the
tortured splash of
incandescent bulbs . . .
from my glassy hotspot I see
angels of darkness in flight
with no compass to locate my condo
shadowed somewhere in the horizon
where-in I've grown weary from
keeping vigils for a dreaded winter
as each day glides past with
expectations of nature's frozen temper.
tonight, I see red in the air for

"Red is freedom road," F. O.[2] said
and red is RATT's Star outlined
by colour blue that reminds
me of hurrying cumulus outside . . .
I will paint the sky red tonight
when the clouds are spread out
like the wings of an eagle in mid flight.
I see floating atop the watery film
of my favourite beverage, pictures of
Edmonton's rousing skyline
but cannot find buried somewhere
in her valley, her river of peace.
at west end, clouds gather like wools
drifting towards this "room at the top."

---

[2] Nigerian playwright, Femi Osofisan. One of his plays is entitled *Red is Freedom Road.*

inside the bar, Edmonton is a chatter of
tongues converging from distant
climes on this dragging Friday night—
but between Power Plant and RATT
there are no signs of Joel with
Bagger, and his advance party,
poets on a mission to pour
libations to their Muse.
now in this suspended bar,
lonely, I wander through a maze
of temptations beckoning
like Irish cream and thinking
of special Thanksgiving turkeys
and the festivities in the air
for tonight I shall paint the sky
inspired by my wrinkled jacket,
a raincoat that reminds me of
the gossamer feel of condoms.
alone in this Edmonton bar
I dream of homeland and
all the guns and crude oil
in combat in the Niger delta.

Hallowe'en Night
(Two voices, to an acoustic guitar)

Ghost-filled silence of a Hallowe'en night,
inside my room, two clocks tick in conversation
like security guards with walkie-talkies,
watchmen for a lonesome poet.

Outside, the oft-busy road is quiet tonight
earth is whitewashed with sandy snow
stretching across fields with its cold glow.
Still, its feathered flakes continue to fall
as if to justify the season's name: Fall.
Sometimes it reminds of the Fall of man—
how Adam proved his love for Eve
and ate of the forbidden fruit. Fall
brings desire to an intemperate lonely
heart craving for that warmth only
Love's fire and lyre can deliver.
I've become a bachelor again,
alien in a material world
separated from family and friends
by demands of the knowledge factory
dispensing wisdom and cant
to a poet with documentary impulse.
It's Hallowe'en night, alright,
and I'm learning new harmonies
of Edmonton's fecund culture, straining
to hear the music of her winds, tonight forgetting
to tender candies to strangers at the door—
children on a surreal seasonal ritual,
screeching like owls and mocking death
with their badly carved Jack-o'-lantern.
Tonight, the TV shows *Inside Hell House*
and a priest calls on every mortal to pray—
"Forgive us our trespasses, Lord,
as we forgive those who trespass against us,
and look not upon our hearts
but upon our humble faith."

But how do I kneel to pray on a Halloween night
when ghosts from another plane crash haunt me?

Nduka Otiono is FS Chia Scholar in the department of English and Film Studies at the University of Alberta and fellow of the William Joiner Centre at the University of Massachusetts in Boston. His first book, *The Night Hides With a Knife*, a collection of short stories, jointly won the ANA/Spectrum Prize. His second, *Voices in the Rainbow*, a collection of poems, was nominated for the ANA/Cadbury Poetry Prize. Otiono is co-editor of *We-Men: An Anthology of Men Writing on Women* and *Camouflage: Best of Contemporary Writing in Nigeria*. He has been a journalist and former general secretary, Association of Nigerian Authors. *Love in a Time of Nightmares*, his most recent collection of poems, from which these poems have been selected, was published in 2008.

REINEKKE LENGELLE
Second Landing

It's an odd thing for a woman who has never been inebriated to tell English speakers that her name sounds exactly like Heineken beer—without the last N of course. And "please replace the H with an R," I say in case I'm speaking to the spelling-impaired. It always gets a chuckle out of the new pronouncer, but if you tested my liver meridian just then, it would be weak.

In 1986 when I returned to Nederland (The Netherlands), the country of my birth, to attend high school, I was so relieved to hear Reineke—the original spelling—read properly off the class list that I committed the moment to memory. After years of being called "Rein-eek" and "Ring-key" and "Ren-i-ca" in Canada, I could just relax. The name isn't common, even in Nederland, but everyone can read and spell it as a matter of course.

The names of my Dutch classmates sounded like this: Maaike, Marita, Marit, Pieter, Erik, Jantien, and Ron (said with a rolling-R). To me the first three names on that list sounded identical and for months I could hardly remember which name belonged to which girl; that's when I realized that foreign names are difficult for the "native" or rather that I had become a foreigner in my native land.

Our emigration journey started in 1975 when my parents moved to Canada and, as Stephen Leacock famously said about his six-year old self, ". . . I decided to go with them." I was just shy of six. Having officially arrived with landed-immigrant status didn't mean that we had completed a successful immigration. What "landing" really means is having a commitment to stay physically and allowing the soul its slower assimilation process. In fact being somewhere fully may be something at which one never fully succeeds.

In Nederland my father was a clinical chemist at a large hospital in Zaandam and we lived in Amsterdam. We had friends there (who could pronounce our names), we went to a good Montessori school nearby, and all our cousins and grandparents lived within a 150-kilometre radius. Geographically this isn't impressive as Nederland fits between Edmonton and Calgary, end to longest end, but for our family it was significant.

The truth is that paranoia brought us to Canada. Maybe for my mother it was adventure-seeking and a desire for change, but for my father it was pure, calculated fear. He had convinced himself during the oil crisis in the early 1970s that the Russians would march into Nederland and put him, the father of four children between the ages of four and eight, under pressure to collaborate with the Communists. He had decided he would have to comply in order to protect us from certain death or oppression; the other option was to simply get out.

Any shrink nowadays could tell you that he wasn't predicting our family's particular fate, instead he was mixing his own childhood war trauma with his mother and father's history—but that's easy to say with confidence in hindsight.

My father's mother, a physician, had stood on the brink of leaving for the United States in the late 1930s but her husband, my grandfather, refused to go. Although she never made it to the States, she did leave my grandfather and her children, including my father who was then only five.

She moved away, joined the Dutch resistance during the Second

World War, and safe-housed a Jewish couple who consequently survived the war. The German officer she was asked to liquidate—in the same house—did not. And what she couldn't foresee was that, despite her steel-nerved acts, the fear she had lived through would be a tense inheritance for the generation ahead. While she left post-war Nederland to live and work in Africa for several years, her son, a quarter century later, would feel compelled to flee Europe in the shadow of the Cold War.

My parents studied the map before they decided where to settle. My father had been in Toronto but found the housing too expensive there. Instead my mother and father eyed Alberta with its natural resources and low taxes. My mother was also drawn to the lush green of Edmonton's river valley.

We arrived in October 1975 and moved into a three-bedroom town-house on the south side of the North Saskatchewan River in the Duggan neighbourhood. My father, feeling he had safely launched his brood, left to "tie up loose ends" and didn't return to settle in Canada until decades later. As if echoing his mother's life, he left his children and marriage, and remained in Europe despite his fear of another war.

It was my mother who had the tenacity and vision to stay in Alberta. Her parents encouraged her to "come home," but she looked forward instead and embraced her life in Edmonton. With tremendous heartache and courage she faced the fact her marriage was over, started her career, and focused on raising us. Eventually she married a man who would become a beloved stepfather.

I didn't realize it trudging through the Edmonton snow; I didn't realize it playing hockey; I didn't fully realize it in junior high where I was the unpopular, flat-chested girl who wore green corduroy pants from the Army & Navy store; but I had not yet fully arrived in Canada.

You arrive in the world as a child of two parents, and you don't land anywhere fully in your life until you are able to literally or symbolically take what you need from both of them. I longed to read and write the language I could hear in my thoughts and could still speak and understand. I longed to walk on the cobbled streets, smell the moist air, and touch the ancient oaks and elms that I couldn't find on the prairies. And most of all I was drawn to be with my father, who I still call Pap (pronounced "pup"). He didn't have to understand that fathers are important for me to understand that truth in my bones. Fortunately, the better chunk of our father-daughter relationship was still ahead of us.

In dramatic teenage style I would say to people (including my mother): I have to go to back to Nederland so I can pick up my soul. I had to bring it back so it could fully inhabit the body that was playing hockey, walking through those snowdrifts, and pledging its oath to the British monarch.

My mother didn't want me to leave Canada. On the other side of the Atlantic my maternal grandparents tried to convince me that vacations with my father were a treat but that life with him on a regular basis wouldn't be. What they didn't realize is that I wasn't looking for a treat. I was looking for *myself*. At age sixteen, I left Edmonton and returned to the country of my birth for what you might call a temporary repatriation.

On the one hand, my arrival in Nederland was met with a warm fatherly welcome and on the other, with the immersion into a somewhat harsh culture. Particularly in the North, the Dutch possess a no-nonsense, tell-it-like-it-is attitude and feel it incumbent upon themselves to tell you whether you're too pale, too fat, too lazy, or too stupid, and they do so with self-righteous verve and not a hint of good humour. While visiting an uncle in the far North, I listened while he—winner of the skunk trophy for positive encouragement to a teenager—told me that the Canadian education was so poor and that I would only be able to do the most remedial level of Dutch high school. He of course, "knew this" because he had seen it with those "poor visiting Americans."

This lowest level of high school in Nederland is where you learn simple bookkeeping and will eventually work as a receptionist somewhere. Or if you're a near dropout by Dutch standards, you'll get training on how to arrange flowers.

The mid-level high school will allow you to become a nurse or teacher or technical something or other—all with further training, of course. The highest level or vwo is the avenue to university and would, my uncle guaranteed, not be open to someone with my dismal background. The evidence seemed to be there: even my Dutch cousins had trouble getting into school at that level. Several of them had climbed painstakingly from level to level.

While my father fretted about how he would get me into the International School, a two-hour train trip from his house, I went off to enrol myself at the local school with my new friend Monique from across the street. I could, after all, still speak and understand Dutch, thanks to my mother's efforts at keeping our language alive at home.

The "conrector" or vice-principal at Grootebroek's Marcus College was Meneer Tim (Mr. Tim). He was a dark-haired fellow with sharp eyes. I could tell from the moment I saw him that he had a built-in shit-detector. I introduced myself and told him I lived with my father a few blocks away and that I wanted to register for school. With some amusement in his eyes, he seriously considered my request.

"What level of schooling do you propose?" he asked.

"vwo," was my unflinching reply. He didn't flinch either.

"And what grade then?"

I told him I had looked at my cousins' schoolbooks and because I didn't really read or write Dutch and my speaking was full of Anglicisms—most of which I didn't notice at the time—it would be best if I started in grade ten again. He smiled and simply said: "Done."

I knew I could keep up in French class as I had taken it since grade three in Canada and math would probably be the same grind as anywhere else. The only subject from which I was fully exempt was "Duits" (German). There would simply be no catching up there, though since then I have learned to order a wiener schnitzel politely in German and book a hotel room—although that is not necessarily a feat to brag about as even Inspector Clouseau can do that.

In a certain sense, I had come home. I rode my bicycle to friends' houses in the neighbourhood and in the surrounding towns and spent time with Pap. I would call him at the lab each day after school, then do hours of schoolwork, cook dinner, and wait for him to get home. Friends came often and played on our saloon-sounding piano, and I had a few sleepover birthday parties with my teenaged girlfriends.

At home we'd always have a lively discussion about some psychological topic and Pap occasionally brought home extra reading for me, one particular book stands out: Alice Miller's *The Drama of the Gifted Child.* It was a text that he felt was required reading for a sixteen-year old.

Miller's ideas, not coincidentally, also spoke to us of our childhood losses. My father also read and translated a medieval Dutch epic—*Floris ende Blanchefloer*—a book I had to study for school. My cousin Jan-Roelof and I drank black tea as we listened to him read, deep into the night.

Afternoons were often spent on the couch studying economics with my dad's girlfriend who dedicated countless hours to helping me study, although the way this subject was handled in Dutch curricula has hitherto been completely useless to me. I did fall in love with Dutch poetry, however, and found it has been part of my soul's work: absorbing the language of my forefathers and mothers. A fond memory I have of Dutch class is finding out that I was the only kid in the room who picked up on the irony in a letter exchange between two Dutch eighteenth-century authors. By the end of my first school year, I even bought my Dutch literature textbooks to the chagrin of local kids who did not understand my enthusiasm for *their* language.

It was obvious to them, and even to me, that despite my immersion back into Dutch culture and school, I remained—a bit proudly, I want to add—Canadian. Though my face shape, long body, and blonde hair were obviously, even stereotypically, Dutch, I noticed that I preferred to write in English and that I kept saying: "I'm only here visiting. I'm actually Canadian."

Not surprisingly the Dutch knew I was a strange bird in their midst. It was the "R" that should be in front of Heineken that seemed to give me away each time. I could not pronounce it consistently like other native-Dutch speakers. You have to roll it on the tip of your tongue (the Scottish can do it) or you have to growl a little near the opening to your throat. If you're feeling a bit lazy the "R" just falls down ("arrrr") and sounds like the "r" in "raven" or at the end of "far."

The Dutch are happy detectives and are so thrilled to find you out. "Your English is very well, very well indeed!" they would proclaim in their pseudo-British accents. (If only they knew that I could identify a Dutch immigrant—who came to Canada in the 1950s by boat—from across a crowded Superstore.)

I skipped out on my graduation ceremony and spent the summer after high school in Edmonton. I returned to Nederland to study at the

Rijks Universiteit Leiden. My father chose history for me and wanted me to study at this oldest of Dutch universities founded in 1575 by Willem of Orange. This monarch had given the university to the people of the town for having resisted the Spanish takeover in the sixteenth century, affirming the people's religious freedom and freedom of speech. Nederland's own Prince Willem Alexander was there studying history himself and this seemed to appeal to my father.

I did not stick with history. After the first day when the professors told us we would need a doctor's note to be absent from a single lecture, I switched majors and signed up for Pedagogy. Heck, I wanted to sleep in some mornings, goof off a bit, and do so on a Dutch-government study grant. I ended up getting my degree in good time and did plenty of creative writing while the professors lectured.

Then the day arrived when I found myself in the KLM office booking my return ticket to Canada. I now knew my pap and my language. I had finished my degree, made friends, and had even had Dutch loves.

Did I miss the space Canada offers or the fresh air or did I want to rejoin the other family group: my mother and siblings? Or was it my father's original mission that I had to be faithful to? There aren't any definitive answers. All I knew was that it was time—my internal clock was moving me forward once again on a different leg of the journey. And my love of Nederland had become somewhat exhausted; this nation that claimed to be liberal, tolerant, and democratic, often felt rule-bound, discriminatory, and simply over-populated.

I remember wanting to take a creative writing course, but I wasn't allowed to enrol unless I had been published in Dutch. I wrote children's stories and even had an illustrator whose work had been published, but to break into the publishing world in Nederland it seemed you had to *know* or *be* someone. And to teach writing was completely out of the question. In Nederland you barely hatch in a professional's eyes until you're forty and even then there is a pecking order. The final straw was that there was about an eight-year waiting list to get an apartment with your own lease and owning your own place was (and still is) prohibitively expensive.

Once I had to leave the house I shared and rented in Amsterdam with my elderly landlady, I declared that I was "one soul too many" in the country of my birth. In the fall of 1995 I flew home to Edmonton, this time skipping out on my university graduation ceremony.

And, this time, I arrived in Canada on my own terms—soul intact. "Landing" for the second time, but this time in a country where *I know* I'm a foreigner, where *I can be* a foreigner and still weep irrationally when I hear the Canadian anthem.

So let's drink to that—foreign beer permitted.

A final note . . . When I left Amsterdam in 1995 I published a small book of poems for my friends and family entitled *Open eyes in bed* (about those quiet, poignant moments when one is alone and reflects on life).

This is one of the poems from that book, which I wrote in both Dutch and English—I'm not sure which language came first.

Amsterdam
Vandaag
hou ik intens
van Amsterdam,
Bij het kruispunt
schieten tranen
in mijn ogen
—heel even
sta ik still bij
HET BESLUIT.
Dan zie de wind
in de bomen–
hier mijn wortels
daar mijn takken.

Today
Amsterdam is
so intensely dear to me,
At the crosswalk
tears shoot to my eyes
—for a moment

I stop and consider
the DECISION.
Then I see the wind in the trees—
here my roots,
there my branches.

Reinekke Lengelle is a published poet, playwright, and self-help author. She has taught creative writing in Canada for more than a decade and is currently a visiting graduate professor with Athabasca University. Reinekke's latest books are *Blossom and Balsam: poems that reveal and heal* (2008), *Blooming Woman : poems & perceptions* (2005), and a self-help booklet called *Bath Oil for Heartbreak* (1995, 2005). Reinekke married Edmonton-born artist Keath Lengle in 1996 and they have two daughters.

MARSH HOKE
Goodnight, America

I am a recovering American. As
they say in the addictions field,
it's a chronic condition from
which one can never recover;
one can only be in recovery. I am
very happy to be in recovery.

I was born in San Antonio,
Texas, in the middle of the
Second World War. My Dad
was a gunnery instructor in the
US Army Air Corps. My mom had come to join him from her home in
Connecticut. After the war was over, we moved back to Connecticut. I
grew up in suburban Hartford, in a pleasantly wooded upper-middle-
class enclave of acreages surrounded by a forest reserve. My family had
lived in that part of the United States for more than three hundred years.
My maternal grandparents lived up the road, and cousins too numerous
to count were close by. I grew up with a strong sense of my good fortune
to be living in the best of all possible places. Inspired by the rhetoric of

post-war progressive Americanism, my patriotism and my faith in the American dream were absolute and unquestioning.

My world-view came apart during the 1960s. I began to be troubled by the hypocrisy inherent in the United States. The "movements"—civil rights, women's rights, anti-war, and anti-poverty—all raised my consciousness. At first, I was a moderate but skeptical supporter of these movements. The ruthless, brutal responses in opposition to them gradually hardened me into a radical. The tear gas, beatings, and even murders directed at youthful idealists were deeply shocking to me. An American Dream I had believed in was revealed to be a sham. Bumper stickers read: "America—Love It or Leave It." I knew what my choice would be. I had entered the 1960s a crew-cut believer. I left them a longhaired, bearded hippy.

During that turbulent decade, I went to university, worked, and did my national service, serving four years as an enlisted man in the US Coast Guard. My progress was not linear, as I flunked out of university twice before finally graduating in 1970. My goals had become clear, though. I wanted to become a social worker—to help those who were struggling.

I met the love of my life, Barbara, in social work school. Early in the summer of 1972, Barbara and I had just received our master's degrees in social work from the University of Maryland in Baltimore, and it was time to look for work. Deeply disillusioned with American society, our thoughts turned north—why not go to Canada, if we could? Perhaps there we would find a better place.

We were living in a cabin in the woods of New Hampshire. As our families had been easterners for many generations, we thought we might as well go west at the same time as we went north. We sent out resumes to every place we could find in western Canada that might hire social workers. After some weeks, we received a message that I was to call Alberta Hospital Ponoka at a certain date and time for a telephone job interview. We had no phone, so I rode my bicycle three miles through the sunny summer forest to a small store by the highway and placed the call from their phone booth. I remember feeling somewhat surreal standing by the road in my cut-off jeans, T-shirt and sandals while I talked to an unknown someone far away who would determine my future. In any case, I guess the interview went well because shortly after Barbara and I were offered jobs at the hospital. We were to start our new positions at the beginning of September.

We had no idea what Alberta would be like. We had family who had visited the Canadian Rockies, but they couldn't tell us anything about central Alberta. "It's flat," said my uncle, who had flown to Edmonton once several years earlier. Would there be any trees? Would we be welcomed?

We packed our worldly goods into a Volkswagen camper in the middle of August—Abel and Oliver the cats, a rocking chair, and two ancient trunks. A small motorcycle was strapped to the front bumper. We left New Hampshire behind and set forth to a new world.

Being Americans still, we drove across the United States before entering Alberta from Montana. Perhaps we were anxious about leaving the old world and entering the new. Our old cat Abel didn't like the prairie— there was no place to hide! He was a city cat from the eastern States, where there were many things to hide from. When we got him out of the van he would slither on his belly through the short grass of eastern Montana, choking on the end of his leash.

We entered Canada August 28, 1972, at Carway, Alberta. At first, the immigration officials didn't want to let us in. Although we had jobs lined up, I had no money because our $350 in traveller's cheques were all in Barbara's name. How would I live until my first pay cheque came through? The regulations said I had to have a couple of hundred dollars to carry me over. Finally, they decided that the VW could be my collateral, and we were in! We were officially landed immigrants in Canada.

As we drove north through the rolling grasslands of southern Alberta, the reality of leaving the homeland of our ancestors began to sink in. I remember listening to Arlo Guthrie's song "City of New Orleans" on the radio. *Good night, America, how are you? Don't you know me, I'm your native son?* I began to cry. I still cry when I think of it—tears for the failed dreams and hypocrisy of America. My family had lived there for nearly 350 years, and now I was leaving.

Someplace between Calgary and Red Deer we began to see trees again. Our spirits lifted, because we are people of the woods and the open prairie grasslands seemed alien. The trees were even thicker around Ponoka, and we camped for our first night in Canada at the highway campsite in the bush near Morningside. That night was cool and dark, with the sky full of brilliant stars. We heard the magical howls of coyotes for the first time in our lives, and we were thrilled to be where we were.

In the morning, we washed our hair under the campground's hand pump. What cold water! It felt like it was hitting the back of our heads with a hammer.

Clean and feeling presentable, we went to the hospital to introduce ourselves. The welcome we received, then and thereafter, was genuinely warm and hospitable. Before long, we knew we had made the right choice.

We lived in Ponoka for two and a half years. We saved our money and then travelled the world for two years. When we came back, we knew that home was now Alberta and that our country was Canada. We moved to Edson in 1977, where we have stayed ever since. We have travelled far away, and even spent two years as overseas volunteers with CUSO, but home is here in west central Alberta. Now, when I've been away and I'm returning west along Highway 16 from Edmonton, I feel a thrill when I see the first spiky muskeg spruce trees sticking up against the blues, oranges, and pinks of the evening sky. Home again. Home at last.

We have never really doubted our decision to come to Canada. Barbara missed the old houses and villages of small-town New England. We both missed the closeness of family and friends left behind. We have made many trips back, to stay connected. We have never missed the society or the culture. The license plates of New Hampshire pronounce the state motto: "Live Free or Die." In New Hampshire, it's illegal to cover up this slogan. Who would want to live in a place like that?

Our last New Hampshire license plate hangs on the old shed that serves as our garage. It reminds me of where I came from and why I left.

We are glad we came to Canada. We found what we were looking for. We left the xenophobic failure of the American Dream, frustrated with the hypocrisy of all those ideals that are stated but not followed. What did we come to? A place with the humility to be unsure of its own identity; a vast landscape of great diversity, where that identity is a work always in progress. That identity rests in the journey, not in the destination, which is always yet to be revealed. This is my home, and I love it.

Marsh Hoke lives in an old log home on the McLeod River outside Edson, Alberta, with his wife, Barbara Prescott. They left Ponoka in 1975 to backpack around the world for two years, then they returned to Alberta. Marsh worked as a counsellor and supervisor with Alberta's addictions prevention and treatment agency, AADAC, in Edson for twenty-five years before his retirement in 2002. For the next two years, the couple worked in Vanuatu as volunteers with CUSO. Now back in Alberta, Marsh teaches anthropology as a part-time instructor with Grande Prairie Regional College. The father of two adult sons, Jonas and Daniel, he is an active cross-country skier, canoeist, and hiker—and he enjoys writing and storytelling.

Rio/Edmonton Non-Stop

Nineteen years ago I arrived in Canada. Edmonton embraced me with a chilly smile on an autumn day. This was my first taste of a strange and unknown country. At that moment, I could not believe that this foreign place would become my home sweet home.

   I had no idea what kind of surprises life would bring me. Coming from Brazil, a tropical country where most of the time we have a summer environment, it was a unique experience for me to learn how to live in the Canadian winter, where some days we could get temperatures of forty degrees below zero. It was beyond my fertile imagination what it would be like to savour the scent of spring, blossoming, full of splendour from the dormant ground. It was magical for me to see nature's transformation in the explosion of fall colours. Everything was an exciting discovery. I felt like a newborn child in a new world: experiencing a new language, meeting new people, tasting other kinds of food, finding a new way to dry clothes, dressing in layers to protect my body against the cold weather, driving on the snowy roads. I was trying to understand the meaning of a new society, an unknown culture where spontaneous hugs or drop-by-for-a-visit-without-a-previous-appointment were not part of daily life. Unfolding each day was a new beginning, a gift that life was giving to me.

I left Rio de Janeiro amidst long goodbyes and a fountain of tears shared with my beloved ones, family and friends. I was always a risk-taking soul, so I had no resistance to opening my wings and flying to the north side of our blue planet. I freed myself to follow my choice with passion and joy mixed with some uncomfortable butterflies in my tummy. I flew into the unknown, expecting life would keep giving me fantastic surprises. I carried no worries in my baggage but lots of empty pages where I intended to write a new chapter of my story.

I had met Laurie in Rio de Janeiro on February 4, 1989. He had left Edmonton three days earlier in the middle of a snowstorm when it was thirty-seven degrees below zero. He landed in Rio on a hot summer day when it was thirty-seven degrees *above* zero, and he was dressed in his warm winter clothes. What a shock for his body! However, I don't think at that moment he realized how much higher his temperature would go during his six months of sabbatical. He had planned to begin his work at the university to coincide with the fun of Rio's famous carnival. Shortly after his arrival my friend Fatima phoned me.

"Hello Thereza? Remember the professor from Canada I told you about, who was coming here for his sabbatical? He is here and is looking for a nice girl to go out with him to the carnival ball at Scala night club. He bought a table for four and a couple from the university is joining him but he would like a date."

"Fatima, my friend," I replied. "I was planning to avoid this carnival. I have some books to read, I want to go to the beach and have some time for myself. Besides, you know I don't speak much English."

"What I know is that you are the right lady for him. You are an exuberant, smiling woman and everyone knows how much you love to dance. Come on! I need your help. Pleeeeeeeease!"

"All right! You got me!"

I don't know how many angels and fairies were participating in my conversation with my friend Fatima, but I believe at that moment they were conspiring to delight me.

Later in the evening I went to Fatima's apartment where Laurie was waiting for me. I was dressed up in a colourful gypsy costume with curious thoughts dancing in my head. When Fatima opened the door I could see Laurie standing beside her with his white Canadian legs exposed beneath a Scottish costume. He kept looking at me with his bright blue eyes, smiling and repeating: "My, oh my, how pretty she is!"

Can you imagine our carnival evening? We danced, we flirted, we drank champagne. I taught him how to move in samba rhythm, and we had lots of fun. The Scala was packed with happy people sparkling in their costumes. The strong rhythmic music, the people's voices singing and dancing freely filled the enlightened space with the joy of living. We couldn't have much conversation, but we raised our glasses with smiles and that sensation of feeling so good. The other couple enjoyed themselves, smiling at us, observing our happiness. We lived a spectacular *folia de carnaval*!

However, a new day arrived and the ball was over. It was four in the morning. Laurie thought it was only an intermission when the band stopped. We wanted to freeze time, to make it stop for us, but life goes on. Our first date seeded a romantic love affair that blossomed into our future life together, but we didn't know that at the time. We decided to enjoy the moment, the present we were having. Laurie's sabbatical became more fiery and frantic than he expected. Having a *carioca* girlfriend, who loved to live life with passion, awakened his wild and adventurous spirit. *Carioca* is the nickname for people who are born in Rio de Janeiro. In the native language of the Tupi people, it means "born in the river."

At the beginning of our relationship we tried to explore the best way to to communicate. Besides my mother language, Portuguese, I had a good knowledge of French and Spanish. Laurie also spoke French although his first language was English. In Rio we managed with mixed languages, words and gestures, a dictionary, and lots of fun. Sometimes we only needed the magical language of love, eye contact, a touch, a smile, or simply a moment together. We discovered how much we could say in silence. We united through our souls.

One week later, Laurie rented a flat in a beautiful place in Rio, called Barra da Tijuca. His apartment was on the twenty-fifth floor with a fantastic view from the balcony. We could enjoy fourteen kilometres of coast and that immense green sea, kissing the white sand of the beach. As soon as he moved into his place he invited me for dinner. He wanted to prepare the meal himself to show me he was a Canadian man who knew how to cook. He told me this later. What he did not know, however, was that in Rio dinner time is much later than he was used to in Canada.

Unaware of this piece of information my enthusiastic professor started to prepare our special dinner at 5:30 in the afternoon. Voila! The chicken went to the oven with salt and black pepper at a low temperature. He peeled the potatoes and carrots and put them on the stove in a pot with water and salt.

Next, he prepared a romantic ambience. He found a candle and improvised a candle holder with a bottle and sat it on the table. He thought it was important to have some drinks to start with and he made the famous Brazilian *caipirinha* made with *cachaca*—strong liquor made of sugar cane, mixed with lime, sugar, and lots of ice. Done!

Then it came six o'clock . . . seven . . . . eight. Where is Thereza? His fearful mind must have been wondering. The chicken went in and out of the oven several times. He wrapped it with aluminum foil and waited. I arrived around 9 PM, a good time to start thinking about having dinner. He welcomed me cheerfully with warm hugs and kisses and suddenly the waiting time disappeared. He showed me his apartment and we stepped out on the balcony to have some drinks while enjoying the twinkling stars and the sea waves dancing on the beach. It was a perfect night for romance. We sat down for dinner. He prepared our plates with the meal cooked hours before. The chicken piece looked quite dark and when I tried to cut it with a knife it crumbled on the plate. We laughed looking at chicken transformed into dark coal. He said that a woman who is able to laugh at a situation like this is the one he wanted to share his life with. Our first dinner story is known by all our friends through Laurie's happy voice.

Time passed faster than we thought, and his sabbatical came to an end. He needed to return to Canada, and I had to stay to attend to my work commitments at the university. On our last day in Rio, Laurie gave me a gorgeous Brazilian bracelet with rainbow colours made with precious stones. It was a symbol of his love and gratitude for our happy time together. Before he left I invited him to return to Brazil in September to attend the wedding of my youngest son. We hugged each other, anxiously looking forward to being together again. After our last good-bye at the Rio airport, we exchanged letters, and phone calls with joyful memories that fed our longing.

September arrived! We were embracing each other again! One week was all we had. Not enough, we knew. There were so many things to talk about, to decide, and we needed to plan our future. Laurie brought an airline ticket so I could go back to Canada with him. I wanted to wave a magic wand to make everything happen as we dreamed but reality reminded me that I couldn't go with him yet. I needed more time to complete the work I was doing. Our decision to be united was strong and final. He left and I was ready to follow him at the end of October. I booked my flight and gave him my day and arrival time in Edmonton. I filled my luggage with my Brazilian clothes while my head filled up with questions that had no answers. I just kept repeating to myself and friends around me: "It's true! I am going!"

I landed in Edmonton on a wet autumn morning. It was Halloween. I was surrounded by friendly witches, I thought. At the airport my boyfriend was waiting with his arms wide open to welcome me. Finally we were together in Canada. The first week was fun visiting new places and meeting some of Laurie's friends. He was taking Portuguese classes with a Brazilian teacher, Ana, who became my friend for life. She was a great help at the beginning with my adaptation to the new environment. During a dinner in a Portuguese restaurant she introduced me to the editor of a Portuguese newspaper in Edmonton, called *The Arauto of Edmonton*. Filled with enthusiasm, I volunteered to write articles for the paper. At that moment I could see some light in my path. I always liked writing poems and stories, and I was searching to do something I liked so I could feel at home.

The time went slowly. Soon I was admiring the beautiful scenery still new to me. Winter arrived. One morning in December, while snowflakes were whitening the pine trees, Alice, the wife of one of Laurie colleagues, phoned me. He had told me previously about her, saying she would call to invite me for lunch. She was curious to meet the Brazilian woman who had won Laurie's heart. I dressed up in Brazilian clothes and a pair of gorgeous high-fashion shoes. When she arrived to pick me up, while hugging and welcoming me, she took one look at my outfit and asked: "Where are your boots, dear?"

When I told her Laurie was planning to give me a pair for Christmas, she laughed and assured me I could not survive a Canadian winter without a good pair of warm boots. We had good time together and after our lunch, she took me to The Bay where I learned how to choose the right pair of boots that would help me survive my first Canadian winter, and many of the following ones.

After the euphoria of the beginning, I found myself feeling blue and very lonely, like a fish out of water. Laurie worked at the university and I was by myself with a new yellow car, which I named Sunshine. I was trying to fit myself into a new world. Soon I realized that romantic love is not the only emotion I wanted to have in my life. I wanted much more than just romance and survival. I wanted to fulfill my own needs and desires. I wanted to feel alive and to express myself freely. But, how? I wasn't able to speak and understand the English language clearly. My Latino blood was boiling to express my passionate soul to the people I was meeting. I kept myself busy most of time writing letters to my family and friends in Brazil, the monthly articles for *Arauto* and writing my desires and frustrations in my journal. When I felt very lonely, the right medication was to phone my beloved ones in Brazil. Later on, when this feeling was gone, I understood what was happening to me. I was suffering from culture shock.

I started to doubt my ability to fit into this new place. I loved Laurie, but what about my soul's expectations? I was lost trying to find an exit door for those dark feelings. Worried about me, and receiving a message from the telephone company about the large long-distance phone bills for calls to Brazil, Laurie decided to invite me for a nice dinner at the Faculty

Club. He held my hands and told me politely that he could not afford to pay those expensive bills every month. I told him how unhappy and sad I was, and how my sadness was hiding the beauty of my soul.

Concerned about my sadness he promised to help me. We didn't want to give up our dream of living together. I always believed in the power of love and in the message: Ask and it is given. We applied for a student visa for me so that I could start taking English courses at the university. My sun was soon shining again. As soon as I began to take the English classes, everything changed. I had a goal to reach: to study and learn English. I was filling my time with creative things to do, meeting interesting people, and doing some volunteer work in the community. Little by little I started to find my place here in Edmonton. It was hard work learning how to find a diamond inside a wild rock, but I found it.

Today when I say I am from Brazil, people ask how I could exchange my tropical city for Edmonton, famous for its cold weather. I always answer with a laugh and say that the art of being happy is a question of attitude. It doesn't depend on warm or cold weather. Warmth and light are within each one of us. The quality of a life depends on how you choose to live. My choice is always to say: Yes.

I took a risk, and I believed I could do it. I knew I could be the woman I am today: ready to give and receive love freely, grateful, expecting a fresh and bright beginning with each new day.

Therezinha França Kennedy taught philosophy, sociology, and history for several years at different schools and universities in Brazil before she came to Canada. As a writer in Brazil, she wrote many distance education courses. After arriving in Alberta, she worked as a writer collaborator for *The Arauto of Edmonton*, a Portuguese language newspaper. She also worked as a tutor of the Portuguese language at home and at the University of Alberta. She is a legal interpreter and translator and has translated several books and documents. She has a passion for writing, loves to travel, dance, and laugh with friends.

SANGMOK LEE

Three Poems

TRANSLATED FROM KOREAN BY MIEUN KWAK

Snow Flower 2

Stars falling over a lone snow flower
    blooming in the winter sky
do my beloved friends look at these stars?
my forgotten childhood memories rise with
    a white heart.
Looking at you aching and gelid, dazzling
    and glittering,
I light up one silver lamp with a longing
    for my hometown.
January is falling in the darkness like a
    white angel.

도시의 그림자

가난이 거미줄처럼
드리운 산 동네에
살아온 연륜만큼
바람도 청정한 날
도시의
짙은 그림자
포도 위에 내린다.

욕심의 두터운 그늘
버리지 못한 내게
모노 필름으로
감고 있는 서울 어디쯤
아직도
우리는 이곳을
달동네라 부른다.

Shadow of the City

In a neighbourhood in the hills
where poverty is woven like a spider web
a day when the wind is pristine
like its life experience,
the dark shadow of the city
falls on the pavement.
I am not able to cast off
the thick shadow of selfishness.
Reeled in a mono film,
somewhere is Seoul,
we still call it Dal-dong-ne, the moon town.

ROCKY 에서

모두가 살아있는 침엽수 밀림 속에서
산 빛을 감아내며 오름 하는 구름들과
여섯 해 그렇게 다가와 눈 뜨는 축복의 산.

빛나던 푸른 여름 돌아보는 자국마다
동면의 나무 가지 톱질하는 바람소리
아직도 차마 다 못 그린 겨울의 하얀 미소.

In the Rockies

In a conifer forest where everything is alive
with rising clouds wrapped around mountain colours
blessed mountains approach me and open their eyes thus for six years
In every detail looking back to the splendid green summer,
there is the sound of the wind sawing the winter tree branches
I still couldn't finish painting the white smile of winter

While working as an architect in South Korea, Sangmok Lee started his journey as a photographer in 1994 and as a poet in 2000. His work and his art have inspired each other in beauty and creativity. He immigrated to Canada in 1998, and he permanently settled in Edmonton in 2007.

Sangmok Lee has established himself as a professional photographer and poet with numerous awards and publications. A member of the Korean Photographers Association, he was selected as a special artist for *Monthly Images*, a well-known photography magazine in Korea. He is also a member of the Korean Writers Assocation. He has published his poetry in *Sijomunhak*, a traditional poetry journal, and later became an editor of this journal. His poetry collection was published in *Samtoh*, a monthly literary magazine, as a special feature in 2006.

Sangmok Lee loves to explore lines, colours, and cultural images in his photography. As a poet, he writes sijo, a purely Korean poetic tradition. Like the Japanese haiku, sijo has a strict form. It consists of three lines with fourteen to sixteen syllables each, for a total of forty-five syllables. Usually the first line states a theme, the second line counters it, and the third line resolves the poem. The lines are divided into groups of three and four syllables separated by pauses. Sijo originated with traditional folk songs almost a thousand years ago, but the modern form has existed for over a century and remains popular. Sangmok Lee hopes to share and express the beauty he sees through his work.

THERESA SAFFA
The Unanswered Question

On a hot sunny morning in March 1993, I embarked on a walk that changed my world view, brightened my horizon, and gave me the opportunity to appreciate myself.

It all started in a small West African state called Sierra Leone, meaning "Lion Mountains" in Portuguese. The population of this country before the rebel war had been between five and six million people, but many people had been killed, displaced, or resettled in other countries like Canada, England, United States, Australia, and many African countries. This was once a peace-loving country, but the advent of the rebel war changed the entire landscape.

In 1992 Alfred, my husband, received a post-doctoral fellowship position to work as a scientist in the Coal Research Centre in Devon,

Alberta. The opportunity came like manna from heaven. At that time Sierra Leone was caught up in a brutal rebel war that had started in 1991 in the far eastern part of the country, on the Sierra Leone–Liberia border, the region where we come from. Everybody was looking for the opportunity to flee the country, but since we were living in the rural area, far away from any border crossing, our journey to Canada was more than a blessing from a Higher Being.

A few months into the war, some of our family members lost their lives, and our part of country was completely cut off from the rest of the country. It was a no-go area and later became the rebel stronghold. We had no access to our relatives. Some fled to Guinea and Liberia, and others were forced to be "head portages" to carry the goods that were stolen from people by the rebels. In a very harsh terrain, through thick forest and bush, over difficult roads, these people had to go with the rebels. They were also used as human shields, to protect the rebels from the advancing government soldiers.

The news of the advancing rebel fighters spread so quickly that we came to the realization that no one was safe. This was a frightening and frustrating situation for us. No place was safe anymore, either, because the fighting was spreading very fast, and the rebels were gaining more ground in the countryside. Life was so uncertain because you never knew where and when they were going to attack.

We were living in constant fear, ready to run or get killed at any time. My husband departed for Canada in early January 1993, leaving the children and me behind. A grief-stricken country was ready to be swallowed up by the rebels at any time. Then came time for me to turn my back away from my weeping country in March 1993.

Firmly holding and pressing the little arms of my five-year-old and my three-year-old, Sia Nde-Nasu and Sahr Makindo, I gave my mom and other family members big, emotional hugs, and with tearful, red eyes I boarded the plane for Canada. Everything we had treasured in life— our family, community, friends, and homeland—was abandoned. We headed for a new home. My mom had always told me to take good care of my children because they are the only rightful possessions we have in the world. I could hear my mother's voice echoing in my head as I left.

My vivid high-school geography knowledge of Canada reminded me of its northern hemispheric location, with glaciated mountains, coniferous forests, and pulp and paper industries, the most famous St. Lawrence Seaway, the warm Labrador Current warming up its coastal areas and the great Canadian Shield. The cold weather was not an issue for us. We only wanted to come to a safe place. That was the picture of my new country that occupied my mind at that time.

As I walked to the plane, I was leaving behind a scene that will haunt me for the rest of my life. When I turned around to wave the last goodbye to my mom and family members, the Lion Mountains, east of the international airport in Freetown, called out to me: *We weep as you leave the Mother Land, the atrocities that will be committed in your absence will forever change the landscape of our beautiful Mother Land, so goodbye daughter of the soil, come back when you can.* This was what I heard the mountains telling me, and indeed everything happened as the mountains predicted. I believe the ancestors were directly talking to me at that time.

My children and I landed as visitors at the Edmonton International Airport on March 22, 1993. The children were excited to see their dad; it was a nice reunion after three months. The immigration officials assisted me with the paperwork at customs, and my exhausted-looking family was escorted to the waiting area where we were met by my husband and his co-worker, Kirk. Not quite prepared for the cold, we were handed winter coats and toques and gloves.

The thought of what I left behind was ever present in my mind. The physical journey had ended, but the emotional and psychological journey continued, especially when the kids kept repeating or imitating the sounds of the different kind of guns that were fired by the warring parties. The children were not immediately aware of the fact that we were in a different and safe country now, so they kept asking about the RUF, as the rebels were called.

My husband's contract ended after two years, but we were able to apply for permanent residency, which was granted, then our new life in Canada began all over again. Another chapter in my life opened in Alberta.

Who am I? A Sierra Leonean, visitor, refugee, or Canadian? This is a question that has pursued me for the past fifteen years. I hope I will be able to answer it some day.

Theresa Saffa, B.Ed., CCDP, works at the Edmonton Mennonite Centre for Newcomers (EMCN) as an accredited level 3 settlement practitioner, career and employment counsellor. She was born and bred in Sierra Leone, West Africa, where she attended both elementary and secondary school and later went to study for a bachelor's degree in Education in the Republic of Ireland.

Theresa went back to Sierra Leone to teach in Njala University Secondary in the late 1980s, where she taught English Language, Geography, and English Literature to senior high-school students. She is married with a son and daughter, ages eighteen and twenty respectively. She left Sierra Leone with her family for Canada in 1993 when the rebel war was at its peak in the country.

In Canada Theresa engaged in a wide range of transitional jobs until she was able to secure full-time employment with EMCN in April 2000. Her main responsibilities include individual employment counselling, outreach employment workshop facilitation, community development, and orientation of newcomers to Canada.

The idea of storytelling and writing began after she participated in a Literacy Day event organized by the Community Development department at the Mennonite Centre. She has been able to translate and tell stories in her native languages; Mende and Creole. Some of her own stories include "The Stranger Who Snored," "Greedy Mr. Spider" and "The Incredible Suitor"; she loves writing folklore and hopes to write a book about herself in the future.

VLADIMIR SILVA
Section Fifteen

Every individual is equal before and under the law and has the right to the equal protection and equal benefit of the law without discrimination and, in particular, without discrimination based on race, national or ethnic origin, colour, religion, sex, age or mental or physical disability.

> —*Section 15, Charter of Rights and Freedoms, Constitution of Canada*

People often ask me about my name. I was born in Peru and Vladimir is not a Spanish name. My mother was a devout Catholic, born in Slovakia. She named me after Saint Vladimir who was the grand prince of Kiev who converted to Christianity in the year 988 and brought the faith to

Ukraine and Russia. Almost a thousand years later, Vladimir Ilyich Lenin did his best to destroy religion in the same part of the world. Believe me, my deeply religious mother was thinking of Saint Vladimir, and not Lenin, when she named me!

I was born in 1952 in the city of Callao, the largest port in Peru. People who live in this city have a nickname—*Chalacos*—and I began my life as one. My father, Juvenal, was a businessman who sold appliances. My mother, Sharolta, was a nurse. I had a brother, Jose Miguel, and that was our family. We moved to another port city, Chimbote, later in my youth because my father thought his business might improve there, and it did.

As a high-school student in Chimbote, and later when I was studying law at San Marcos University in Lima, I began to read novels as a way to learn about the world. I loved the Peruvian writer Mario Vargas Llosa first, and perhaps the most, because he touched forbidden topics that a young man would want to know more about. He wrote about women, sex, and people who lived in a different and more exciting environment than I knew at the time. The book I loved most was *La Casa Verde* (*The Green House*). He wrote about places like the Mangancheria neighbourhood in Piura, and Santa Maria de Las Nievas, Iquitos, River Amazonas, and he described them so well that he transported me there. I wanted to go myself to see these places, and I still do. Someday, perhaps, I will.

I graduated from the university, and practiced criminal law for about five years. Then the economy in Peru started to deteriorate. It got very bad. People had no money so they bypassed the services of a young lawyer. At the time, I didn't have a job with a company, or with the government, which would have changed my situation a bit. I worked in a small firm with two other lawyers. We had a very difficult time.

My brother had moved to Edmonton where he found a job in the construction business. He told me to come to Canada, that I would do better here, so I decided to try my luck in this country.

I arrived in Alberta in 1986. I was 34 years old. I came here when I was too old, and that's a fact. I learned that in time. I might have done better if I had come here as a younger man. However, I did start to work here right away. I found a job as a security guard, and I thought that was fine because at last I was earning some money. Although I had known a little English in Peru, I had to work hard here to improve my English. I studied the language in many classes, at Edmonton Immigrant Services Association, at the Edmonton Mennonite Centre for Newcomers, at Catholic Immigrant Services, at MacEwan College, many classes. One teacher allowed me to attend half-days in her classes because I worked at night.

I will be honest. At the beginning I wanted to go back to Peru because I missed my family, my many relatives, and my friends. When you decide to leave a country, you don't stop to think about the people you are leaving behind. Once you arrive in the new place it is lonely to live without them. I guess that would happen to anybody. If you moved to Peru, it would probably be the same for you.

I came here alone, but I had a girlfriend in Lima—Andrea—and I missed her. I went back, and we got married, and then we returned here. Since then I have not been back to Lima for twenty years.

My wife and I found some old friends at the Edmonton Public Library, on the bookshelves. We found the writers we loved and their books in Spanish. I read Alejo Carpentier, Gabriel Garcia Marquez, Mario Benedetti, J. M. Arguedas, Ciro Alegria, Ricardo Palma, Cesar Vallejo, Luis F. Angell, Augusto Roa Bastos, Ernesto Sabato, and so many other good ones. We read Canadian writers, too, from Emily Murphy and her story of platonic love to Ted Byfield and his politics, with many writers in between. The library was my good friend, and it became a good connection for us to the city itself.

As for my life in Edmonton, I worked at different jobs as the years went by. First as a security guard, later I was a caretaker, and after that a cab driver. Then, about seven years ago, my health began to be a big problem. I have a serious heart condition, with very high blood pressure, and I had to retire. I wanted to do something, not only to fill the time but also to make my life interesting and useful. I began to write.

It happened like this. One day I was reading a terrible book. I won't tell you the author or the title, but I slammed it down and said to myself: "If that author can find a publisher for that book, I am sure I can do better."

You see, I had the dream of becoming a writer when I was a much younger person. Yet when I was young, I didn't have too much to say, and I didn't have the words to say it. When I became older, I had more life experience, more ideas, and I had read more books, magazines, and newspapers. I felt I could express myself with more confidence and I also had more stories to tell to the world.

Four years ago I began a novel. I was living in Edmonton so I decided the story should be set in this city. And I wanted the characters to be young. My novel is about three teenagers in Edmonton—two young men from Vegreville named Peter and Paul, and a young girl from the Enoch Cree Nation named Sara. They come to the city and get to know each other and experience some upheavals in their lives, and eventually get in trouble with the law. At the same time, there is a parallel story about two immigrants, Surinder from India and Julia from Peru, and their struggles. They do not encounter the other three teenagers until the epilogue. All of these characters live in small apartments one block away from each other, around 107th Avenue where I used to live.

At first, this story was just an enjoyable way to fill my time. I kept adding pages. The pile of loose pages grew higher and higher. The characters woke up on the page and became interesting. I started to appreciate them. They became real people to me.

I wrote my novel by hand in English. At that time I didn't own a computer, and I also didn't know how to use one. Soon I had three hundred pages of hand-written work. I said to myself: "This could be a book. This could be my contribution to Canada. People might say, 'This guy gave something to the country. Maybe he didn't with the rest of his work, but look at this book he gave us.'"

I began to attend a writers' group at the library on Sunday afternoons, and later I joined a smaller group of writers at the library who came to Alberta from all over the world. Some of these new friends are publishing their stories and poems in this book. I have only recently started to show my own writing to other writers. One good friend read my manuscript, and she suggested that I write the story again in Spanish, my original language, so that my imagination could be entirely free to express itself in the language I know best. So I did that. Writing by hand again, all three hundred pages, I started from the beginning and translated the whole book from English into Spanish. This turned out to be a very good idea. It is a much better book now. I can say things with so much more variation, so many more feelings and ideas, in a descriptive way, and I make fewer errors in grammar. For example in English I might write: "The girl got sat in the chair." *La chica sentose en la silla.* That sounds better. I remain in doubt about the title. In Spanish it is *Chabacaneria.* In English it would be, *A Clumsy Job,* but I'm not sure if the words are exactly right. I will continue to consider the matter.

The challenge, of course, is that now I have to translate my book back into English! I want the book to be published in English, but I am also thinking about my characters and their city. They speak English and they live in Edmonton. Can you imagine a Canadian-born teenager from Vegreville walking down 107th Avenue speaking to his friend in Spanish? For him and the others, I need a translator. So I need to find somebody first to put the story into a computer, then I need to find a translator, then I need to approach a publisher. And I know zero about publishing.

I am not frustrated. I am older. I understand that some things can happen and other things cannot. Things are like that. I always keep a little hope alive that my book will be published in Canada. I have plans for this story. I want to talk to young people in an interesting way about the problems of getting in trouble with the law. The other thing, I guess, is that I want to say something about Canada and immigrants, and our society. I know people born in Canada should be treated well. They inherited this nation from their parents and grandparents and ancestors. I appreciate that, and I understand it. I could add that when you have enough, when your lives are good, then you should try to treat immigrants, well, too. You have to see the big picture. The big picture should include all of us. There should be only one picture.

The section I like best in Canada's constitution is section fifteen. It is magnificent. I always remember it. It says everyone is equal. The key word is everyone. I like that. I think it's great. I want to express my gratitude to Canada for my time here and for this opportunity to write and express my ideas. It is important to recognize when something good has happened to you. For me, writing my story in this book has been something good.

Vladimir Silva continues to search for a translator and editor who can help him transform his hand-written novel into a published book in Canada. He has volunteered for Meals on Wheels and the Food Bank, and he and his wife, Andrea, also volunteer with the Language Bank at Edmonton Immigrant Services Association. They live in downtown Edmonton.

IKPONWOSA "I.K." ERO AND COMFORT ADESUWA ERO

Pieces of a Journey: An E-mail Memoir

This is a story about my mother and about me, about our individual and yet shared experiences on our journey to Canada from Nigeria twelve years ago. Our collaborative story is shaped in the form of dialogue conducted via e-mail between Edmonton and Vancouver. We each wrote our own sections except for the last, which is an amalgamated conclusion.

Recalling our journey in one piece was an enlightening process for me as I came to understand more fully that my story began with my mother's. Although this realization might sound trivial to some, it is not something that I had taken for granted. I had assumed, for the most part, that my journey here involved my own consciousness and my solitude.

So it is with great appreciation that I acknowledge that this dialogue

with my mother opened an even larger dialogue that explored the generation gap between us and anchored my journey in a larger context.

—I. K. Ero, Edmonton, 2008

Dear Mommy,
Do you remember those days?
When we had it all: cars, a nice house and yes, money.
Everything was cheap, life was expectant.
Do you remember
beautiful neighbours with their exaggerated yet entertaining gossip,
Delivered hot, spiced with enthusiastic gesticulations,
stories sworn true by the wide eyes of the teller?
Do you remember those days when the dust of *harmattan* meant
    Christmas
while the journeys from town to village meant New Year
And the sound of the pestle rhythmically in sync with mortar meant
    a heavy meal of *foofoo,* to be accompanied by sweet-smelling
    spinach stew?
Do you remember?

Mommy:
Yes I do; Oh yes I do remember, my daughter.
Life in the village
Even before I conceived you.
I remember
And for all around you, lend your eyes, your mind, and ear
Oh yes I remember it all too
It all began when I was a child in the village
Being part of a chief's household
We were all part of the whole village
And the village was part of us all
It was satisfaction galore as we made do with
What we had in nature
We planted and reaped, manufactured and decorated with
All items of nature, leaves, plants, wood, twines, clay, beads all

But what actually held me in awe
Were the stories told by the wise, the mamas and all
Tales filled the air.
Legends made us proud of those past
Griots, travellers and itinerant workers all were welcomed with
    warmth
And greeted with familial goodbyes as they left behind the perfume
    of their experience
And the music from their hearts.
I remember the sparkling village river
Gargling and gurgling at the tales we told
And the games we played as we swam
And Oghan, our mother river, embraced us and bathed us in its
Cool and shimmering depths embedded with crystal-like grainy sand.
Then I remember the day I was torn away to go to the city to school
I felt I was torn off at my roots.
The heart and soul nourishing roots of my native village
The land of my birth.
The journey took me to new places, new schools of new experiences,
    new friends, new love, new job, and a marriage!
Like in a mirage, the informal schooling of my village remained
in my heart like the indelible dye of the indigo leaves.
Then you and your siblings came along, my daughter.
I yearned to share my evergreen village experiences with you
Yes I am happy you remember the village trips
that immersed you,
the indescribable and soul-binding physical and spiritual experience.
The yams, the spicy stews, the sound of the pestles, the cool *harmattan* wind, harbinger of the festive-filled village New Year!
Yes I remember; Oh yes I do!

Daughter:
Do you remember when
Fear gripped the entire nation
Accompanied by the feeling of pain, the feeling of hopelessness

And worst of all, the feeling of loss?
Old things took on new meanings.
The neighbours' gossip was now political chatter or worse still
A plea for food, water, or some other commodity already rationed
    in our home.
Yet we gave, relying on the heavy intangible hope that tomorrow
    would improve.
At other times, there was unexplained adult panic:
you and other parents would rush to get us from school,
once a year, then later twice or three times a year.
Green leaves adorned your Peugeot 504.
Sweat and anxiety adorned your motherly yet youthful face.
"There's a riot in town! Get into the car!" you would say.
Somehow we knew the chaos would pass,
yet somehow we also knew its passing would deposit residues
that would slowly sediment into a political deadlock.
Life would soon be difficult.
Mommy, do you remember?

Mommy:
This puncture in our bubble of security was as sudden as lightning.
In the year 1966, long before you were born, we were asleep in the
    dorm of a high school when:
"boom, boom, crack, boom, boom, boom!" came a terrible sound as
    ground shaking as the angry roar of a lion.
"Quick, crawl under your beds!" ordered our panicking and
    dishevelled nun teachers and guardians.
Without questioning, we obeyed blindly, our hearts pounding
    heavily against our rib cages.
"It is a military coup," they announced to us the following day. "The
    military men, the soldiers, have taken over power and government
    in your country. You all have to be sent home at once."
This was the beginning of our woes in the country, my daughter
About thirty years of military rule.
You were born right in the middle of the rule of the gun-toting,

order-barking, iron-helmeted men in power.

Our people say: "Let no one uproot the pumpkin from the old homestead." The iron-helmeted, gun-toting men did uproot the pumpkin and what happened?

Yes, I remember the chaos, the suffering, the insecurity, a hopeless situation, the arrests, threats, senseless killings, coups and counter coups, the silencing of the peoples' voices, the deliberate attempt to kill the will of the people. What is more, all were impoverished. Our culture was thrashed and bastardized.

Jobs were done but people were not paid as the spitfire khaki-wearing ones siphoned the honey from the belly of our oil-rich mother land.

Daughter:
Things must have gone from bad to worse
Because even though I was born into military rule
I recollect better days.
Yet how things went bad strikes a louder chord in my memory.
Oh yes, I remember the downturn
The dust of the annual *harmattan* became annoying.
It beckoned a Christmas that no one could afford
Trips to the village now happened only in my mind's eye.
I can hear grandmother singing in the open air kitchen of the village.
I can see my little cousins, scantily clad, playing in the red dust of
    the earth.
I can see them all in my memory, memories intermittently interrupted
by the sound of your mortar and pestle in the kitchen,
Only this time, it is not *foo-foo*.
It is another of mommy's invented meals,
Concocted in the national heat of necessity.
Mommy, do you like to remember?

Mommy:
Yes I do but I hate to remember this part.
My children, not fully aware of the economic situation

Refusing to eat concocted corn and cassava meals
Or concocted bitter malaria medicine
When authentic drugs were not available or unaffordable
I stop the remembrance of this part because it will tear any parent's
    heart apart!

Daughter:
As the leaders of a nation fought, people suffered.
Indeed until then, I never paid attention to the words of our elders
But now I see: "When elephants fight, it is the grass beneath their
    feet that suffers."
I understand: "There is nothing beautiful about war."
And: "You must not be hungry if you refuse to eat an unfamiliar meal."
And we waited for respite from the heat of uncertainty.
We longed for the heavenly pin that would deflate our currency
    swollen without value.
We ached for what wasn't
Our memory's attempt to restore what once was
Supplied our breath, and nurtured our culture.
The political warfare turned against writers,
Journalists and vocal persons.
Mommy, your manuscripts were stuffed in boxes, stowed away in
    storage.
Today your friend has been arrested for writing,
tomorrow another friend is no longer trusted,
Word has it that she works as a government spy
And she knows mommy writes.

Mommy:
And Churches prayed, Mosques preached, traditional healers gave
    offerings to the gods of the land to save us from the plague of
    military rulers. Some bold activists took to the streets and were
    gunned down or clamped in prison. Students rose up in protest
    and were mowed down. Writers decided to use the pen. You
    know very well that this did not work

Daughter:
Mommy, do you remember when
Months of bleakness rolled into years of darkness?
But we still saw the light in the far distance
Our march towards it was slow, pained and yet determined.
We marched as a family, yet we could hear the steps of a multitude
    around us
A nation marching towards the light in the distance
This was our psyche. We had no other choice.
Our hope soon incarnated.
The phone rang one humid Thursday evening.
It was big sister studying on scholarship in Canada.
"Hello," she says, "I have good news!"
Mommy, you paused on the other end of the phone.
Big sister goes on, "Canada gives people like us, fleeing injustices,
An opportunity to come here as a family."

Mommy:
But before our good news materialized. I went to France for a
    course. I decided to stay back at the end of the course. Things
    happened very fast for us.
First I received the permit to stay in France for ten years. Then
    my daughter in Canada wanted us to move to Canada. My first
    interview in Paris gave my children and me landed immigrant
    status in Canada. Like lightning, my children's papers went
    through and like in a trance they joined me in France and we
    found ourselves soon after in C A N A D A!

Mommy and Daughter:
We landed in Canada approximately twelve years ago from Nigeria.
We remember!
We hugged our hand luggage so tight. It was the only tangible piece
    of our past that we could possess—so we thought anyway. Ha!
The memories of our journey to this vast North American
    country are beginning to resurrect and we will, by writing

and reminiscing, take possession of these memories as the true
tangible part of our past.
after years of silence about our journey here.
we summon the courage to remember it all
we will come to terms with a painful journey
hope brought forth joy to us
and the journey will bring more joy to our descendants
with whom we hope to share the story that brought us here.

Ikponwosa Ero, the daughter in this dialogue, was born nearly thirty years ago in the city of Ibadan, Nigeria to two teachers: one of the sciences and one of the arts. I. K. is the fifth of six children, all of whom have immigrated to Canada. She arrived at the age of fifteen and feels privileged to have access to both Nigerian and Canadian worlds.

At the heart of I. K's passion is humanitarian and human development work. She has participated in the activities of the Unveiling Africa Foundation, Edmonton, The Nigeria Association of Edmonton, and The Advocates for Sight Impaired Consumers, among others. As a strong supporter of arts in the community, I. K. has stage-managed several productions and festivals including *One Heart, One Voice* (2008), *Izabobo* (2007), Collingwood Days Festival (2005), and *The Dance of the Leopard* (2003). She has a master's degree in development and looks forward to continuing her academic studies, as well as expanding her artistic experiences both in writing and in the performing arts. She lives in Edmonton.

Comfort Adesuwa Ero, the mother in this dialogue, was raised in a Nigerian Bini chief's household where tradition and culture are passed on to the child by the ever-present grandparents, uncles, aunties, and cousins who all live within the same household. Comfort has learned and told folktales and songs ever since she learned to talk. She studied languages and drama and became a teacher at a time when it was very unpopular in Africa to send girls to school. She has a BA in French, postgraduate diploma in Education, a master's degree in Education; and is a certified teacher in British Columbia. Comfort has over thirty years of experience as a classroom teacher and principal in both Nigerian and Canadian high schools and colleges. She is currently the artistic director of African Stages Association of BC.

She is the author of a novel in French, *La Fuite*; a children's book, *Kokodiko: The Dance Monster*, and she has contributed oral stories to the Vancouver Society of Storytelling CD projects. Comfort's most recent theatre productions include *Seeds of Respect*—a youth anti-bullying performance in collaboration with the Canadian Red Cross (2008) *Izabobo!: Celebrating Rythyms in the Circle of Life* (2007); *Macbeth is African* (2007); *The Lioness Can Also Roar* (2006); and *The Dance of the Leopard* (2003). She lives in Vancouver.

Ishaa & Me

I came to Canada in June of 2002. I thought I would only be visiting my husband for three months, after which I had planned to return to my work in India. Little did I know that I had arrived in Canada to start a new life with my newfound family: Naveen, my husband; Anand, my stepson; and Ishaa my thirteen-year-old daughter from a previous marriage.

I had met Naveen at my daughter's boarding school in India. He was Ishaa's new music teacher who also taught science to the junior-high kids. I thought this combination was very appealing and found myself becoming attracted to this Indian-born Canadian who had left his job in Canada to teach in a boarding school in India with the hope of raising his son as a single parent. We shared the common dream of bringing up our teenage kids as a family. We got married and soon after he left for Canada, since his son who was raised in a Western environment couldn't adjust to the communal lifestyle of the school. A year later, I followed him.

Ishaa joined us six months after my arrival. She was excited to embrace the new environment in Canada, the land of opportunity, the idyllic Western world. It was all very appealing to the young mind; as for me, I was still resisting fitting in. At the back of my mind I intended to return to India. I was not feeling in control, and I felt very inadequate in my new setting. I had lost my original identity, that of filmmaker, and I had to assume a new role—full-time mother and wife—in short, the role of the homemaker. It was like being in a movie; it seemed unreal, yet it was all actually happening. I was not mentally prepared to receive my new environment in its entirety. It was a struggle at various levels: my accent, making new friends, rediscovering my identity, appropriate social behaviour, to name a few.

On the other hand, I saw my daughter Ishaa willingly embrace her new life in totality—the accent, the cultural nuances, and the peer pressures. I could see she was happily assuming a new identity. She was willing to go the whole nine yards so that she would fit in among her new friends. I suppose when you are younger, you can absorb changes around you better, or so I thought at that time. It was not until Ishaa started going to school that I observed the vast gap between her and her classmates. I could see her struggle, but I was unable to be of any help. I was struggling with my own adjustment. The gap in peer expectations and levels of awareness between Ishaa and her peers in Canada and India was vast. It wasn't going to be easy for this young pre-teen. I could see her change in leaps and bounds. The transformation was not gradual and organic, it was a radical change from a naïve preteen to a rebellious teenager. The change was too drastic for me to handle—it was like Ishaa had grown into a young adult overnight. She was making her own decisions without consulting me; my rules made no sense to her; her dress sense did not appeal to me; she couldn't care less about my opinion. I started to feel that I was losing my power as a parent. I didn't know how to react to the New Ishaa—my only concern being, was it for the better or for the worse?

In her new environment, as Ishaa embraced the challenge to do whatever it took to fit in, my fears were confirmed. I was drifting away from my daughter, who was growing rapidly into a culture diametrically opposite from mine. I began to function in panic mode: I tried to hold her down, reminding her at every turn about her roots, her values and customs. I was regulating the shows she could watch on television. I even asked my mother to come and stay with us, so Ishaa wouldn't lose her culture and language.

I soon realized that the conflicts were impenetrable so I started "backing off," a term Ishaa used often while speaking to me.

I strived to find my balance through film. I started observing Ishaa like a subject: the subject of a film I wanted to make with her. I videotaped her whenever I could, saved her telephone messages, made her speak to me candidly, and made my notes on the transformation she was undergoing. On her part, Ishaa started discussing an idea for a film documentary with me on the theme of popular kids, which she wanted to call "Race to Popularity." This sharing of ideas, thoughts, and feelings without being judged brought Ishaa closer to me. At that point, she was unaware that I was planning a film with her, and I was unaware of the healing that was naturally taking place as a result of our conversations. Unwittingly, I was slowly beginning to embrace my new environment . . .

While I was still battling to assert my position in my daughter's life, I became pregnant. I was going to be a mother all over again. When I shared the news with Ishaa, she was very happy at the prospect of having a little brother or sister. Nine months later, Ishan, my baby boy came along. Ishan became a neutralizing factor in our lives. I was less overbearing and Ishaa began to shower all her love on this little bundle of joy. Early in my pregnancy, she had written in her diary:

> I was so happy I forgot to thank god but I decided not to be rude. That night I cozily crept into my blanket and slowly closed my eyes and thanked god for the wonderful gift he was about to deliver to us. It does take time. I mean, I heard myself saying "can't you hurry it up man?" I can hardly wait, uuuurrgghhhh, 9 months!!! Who u kidding????" but I guess my mom needed those nine months u know. I mean after that there would be like a pain in the ass for the rest of her life, hehehe, just kidding . . .

One day as I was waiting to pick Ishaa up from school, I saw a huge crowd of teens emerging from the school building. I was very intimidated! This is what Ishaa was confronting every day. I was crushed and my heart ached for my daughter's own secret struggle to become part of her new setting. At this point I changed my own behaviour and expectations of my child. I tried to reach out to her. She revealed that her Indian peers in Edmonton were not like her pals back home, meaning that they were completely part of the Western world, totally unaware of the Indian sensibility and culture. She revealed to me that she did miss home, that she did not want to forget her roots—her culture, her ethos, her language, in short, her heritage. She tried to keep all of this alive through her choice of school assignments. She chose India and Indian themes as part of her class research work because she wanted to share that experience with her peers. Later that changed. She realized that her peers were not interested in her "homesick stories."

It was not until Ishaa entered high school that she strongly articulated her yearning for home. I wanted her to complete high school first, after which she could return to India. Sometimes we don't take seriously the messages our children constantly give us, directly or indirectly, through their behaviour and brazen expression of feelings. The final crisis took place in the summer after Ishaa completed grade ten. She forced us to consider her feelings seriously. As a family we made the decision to help Ishaa make the journey back home. So in January of 2008, I took Ishaa, along with little Ishan, to India. We moved to Pune, a growing city close to Mumbai and decided to set up a home there. It at once became evident to me that this is where Ishaa belonged. How unusual was this! I was the one who had initially resisted "fitting in," but it was Ishaa who continued to feel uprooted and could never forget her connection with the Indian soil.

Today I find myself in a more fluid situation. I am more accepting of changing scenarios in my life. No matter where I am, I will never fully belong either to India or Canada, nor will I ever completely be either Canadian or Indian! Such is the price of immigration. It is an irreversible condition that leaves you with a diffused identity.

It has been a huge learning curve for me as a mother to raise a teenage daughter in a new culture. Now I am all geared up to raising little Ishan in Canada as a Canadian-born Indian. I want him to be proud of his cultural heritage, and at the same time I want to allow him the space to become the person he wishes to be. The answer to the question "Who am I?" is not an easy one. It is a journey for every child—always growing, evolving, changing, and surprising us along the way.

A famous quotation from Kahlil Gibran's *The Prophet* stays with me:

Your children are not your children.

They are the sons and daughters of Life's longing for itself . . . You may give them your love but not your thoughts. For they have their own thoughts . . . You are the bows from which your children as living arrows are sent forth.

Shabnam Sukhdev is a filmmaker in Alberta and India. After completing her studies at the Film & Television Institute of India (FTII), Pune, with a diploma in film direction in 1994, she worked in the media arts industry in Mumbai as a writer, director, and producer of television shorts, movies, and documentaries. Shabnam immigrated to Canada in 2003. Her work in Alberta includes *Stranger In My Own Skin*, a film portrait of the poet Iman Mersal; *Veiled Voices*, a documentary about women in Edmonton's South Asian community; and *Machos: Journey of Self-discovery with Immigrant Men*. She and her family members divide their time between homes in Edmonton and Pune.

PETER MIDGLEY
Four Poems

ichanti strays far from home

What is this strange creature?
Perhaps it is *ichanti*, the watersnake
    with its many colours writhing
around the country, ribs articulated
railway sleepers.
Ah, if it is *ichanti*,
this creature is far from home . . .

There it is.
There it is with its articulated cars linking
into flimsy backbone
anaemic white bones
clasping a continent.

Backbone! It's good to have a backbone!

Indeed, it's good to have a backbone!
Madiba: now he has a backbone.
a backbone, I tell you, so strong they piled
27 years of shit on it;
so broad comrades could walk from Robben Island on it.
They could cross the ocean on the *ithambo* highway
proud as *ingxa-ngxosi* carrying its prey.

Now what is a person without a backbone?
I ask again: what's a person without a backbone?

Aaah! . . . ndiyabona!
Ndiyabona madoda ne abafazi
I see you, men and women
I see you sitting in your chairs
sheltered inside comfortable cabooses,
watching your country outside being stolen.

That *tjoek-tjoekmakgala* thingy
carries out diamonds and gold
in its belly. Those little cars strung like vertebrae
on the track snake across the country, grabbing.
That snake settles around your necks, strangles people.

There you are: hiding in your cabooses.
Sitting right inside this beast
wearing those bloody diamonds.

Send them back, I tell you. Send them back!
Send *ichanti* back to its watery hole
Show your backbone!
I've said enough, I'll say no more.[1]

---

[1] *ithambo*: bone. The plural, *amathambo*, refers to the bones of the ancestors. It is also a pun on Oliver
  Tambo's name.
ingxa-ngxosi: Secretary bird.

paging through my photo album

i.
josef
tall and lanky ovambo man beside my small figure on the grass
taught me
my first words
in oshiwambo
of you I remember

only: *wau penduka*
hurry slowly

then you left
back home to a reserve north of Okahandja
to wait for the next labour
contract
and a new family
not your own

ii.
you of the unknown name, maker of family legend
you kindly commented on the protruding barn doors: *hy't potlood-ore*

how true your prophecy: for like a secretary bird
I fold feathered thoughts behind oblong ears
forge them into written images

iii.
mary matyobeni, nontombi
forever standing beside the back
door singing: *yihla moya*
come, oh spirit
ed one

squinting Xhosa phrases into the midday sun
turned my skin a nutty Tembu brown

iv.

molefe the school janitor's gifts: a frank talk
in the boiler room infiltrated by township smells
dog-eared smoky lines
permeate the childhood mind: *Morena boloka*
sechaba sa heso

and outside the cadet drill sergeant
shouts conscientiously—youth
preparing youth for the total onslaught

note to self: skipping class—a transgression
punishable by detention[2]

---

[2] *hy't potlood-ore*: "He has pencil-ears." He has ears you can rest a pencil on easily; he's a book person.
yihla moya: "Come, o spirit." An isiXhosa phrase taken from the South African national anthem, "Nkosi
   sikilel' iAfrika."
Frank Talk: the name of a magazine edited by Stephen Bantu Biko before his murder at the hands of the
   police.
Morena boloka sechaba sa heso: The Sesotho words to part of the national anthem. Loose translation: "God
   bless Africa." *Sechaba* was also the name of the ANC's underground magazine.
To avoid attending "Moral Preparedness" classes, I used to hide in the school boiler room, where I
   secreted copies of *Frank Talk* and *Sechaba*. Since these were banned publications, mere possession
   of them was a criminal offence. "Moral Preparedness" (also called, more bluntly, Cadets) was a
   compulsory subject in which young white South Africans learned military drills, practiced shooting and assembling R-4 rifles, and learned to identify explosive devices.

miskien moet ek . . .

miskien moet ek 'n nuttelose gedig skryf
sonder seks   sonder liefde   sonder politiek
sonder 'n verlede
stomgeslaan   blote papierwoorde
om my woedende tong te streel   en hom dan
opvou soos 'n jet
en in sy moer in stuur

perhaps i should write an utterly useless poem

without sex   without love   without politics
without a past
dumbstruck   mere paper-words
to caress my angry tongue   then
fold it into a paper jet
and oh, to hell with it

eerste indrukke

ek het begin skryf
in my kop sê ek toe op:
vandag het ek my eerste ekster gesien
swart en wit en skimmel-
mooi in vlug . . .
en soos hy styg, kon ek
winter sien aankom soos 'n koue ster
net daar het die gedig gevries
summier grond toe geval:
morsdood
hy't seker ook maar Afrika gemis

first impressions

i started writing a poem
in my head it read:
today i saw my first magpie—
black and white and iridescent
in exuberant flight . . .
as it rose, i saw
winter approach like a frozen star
in that instant the poem froze
dropped to the ground:
dead
probably because it missed Afrika too

Peter Midgley was born in Namibia and raised there and in South Africa's Eastern Cape Province. He is a storyteller and writes children's stories, plays, and poetry. His plays have been performed in South Africa and Namibia. Peter came to Canada in 1999 to do a PhD and ended up staying longer than he intended. He lives in Edmonton where he is managing editor at University of Alberta Press.

Golden Birds and a Chess Set

I am an artist and a poet in my heart, although not too many people know this. I write in Vietnamese or in English when the feelings come to me.

I was born in 1950 in Can Tho, a city with a beautiful name. *Cam thi giang* means "river of music and poems" in Vietnamese. When I was young, I loved to go to the country-side. My grandmother would come to the city on Saturday afternoon to take me to her farm, then bring me home in time for school on Monday morning.

My grandfather had a very interesting philosophy of life. He explained proverbs to me. He made special time to talk to me. I liked to stay close to him and his elderly friends when they sipped tea, played chess, or recited poetry at night. He was not a strong Buddhist, in the sense that he didn't go to the temple and do the chanting, but he lived according to the principles of Taoist philosophy. He said we had to train ourselves to be good people and to live in harmony with the world. He also told me: "When you are angry, find a way to say it indirectly to keep a peaceful atmosphere." I learned to be silent.

My love of art began in my time with him. My grandfather taught me to look at the beauty in front of me—in a bird, a fish, a tree—and to allow it to come into my language and into my hands. At school, I used to steal the chalk and carve small figures of legendary animals.

The years of my youth brought heavy and violent war across Vietnam. It did not physically hurt my family but we were fearful. I witnessed the wounded soldiers and civilians; I heard that friends and schoolmates had been killed. I continued to go to school, and I graduated from agricultural college at the hardest time of the war. I was busy in those years, volunteering with literacy programs for the families of the poorly educated mothers and children who wanted to read the letters from their husbands, fathers, and sons who were soldiers. I married my husband in 1973. My relatives suggested to us that we should leave the country as soon as possible. My husband and I decided to wait until our son was born.

My first son was born in April just before the fall of South Vietnam to the Communists on April 30, 1975. The opportunity for us to leave finally came in 1978. We paid all of our savings to leave Vietnam and travel by boat to Malaysia. We stayed in a refugee camp for about three months.

We had no choice about our destination country. At the camp, we lined up to be interviewed. My family was accepted to go to Edmonton, Alberta. I knew a little about Canada. I knew it was the coldest place in the world. I pictured it like the scenes in the movie *Dr. Zhivago*. We flew into Vancouver in a small group of twelve people. On my first day in Edmonton, it was twenty-one degrees below zero. I had bought a warm jacket in Malaysia for Canada, but it was not warm enough to wear in Edmonton. Both my husband and I wore dress shoes. I saw him slipping and sliding on the icy sidewalk. I was so frightened of the cold. It was hard on my spirit. It was not as beautiful as in the movie.

I was able to speak and write in English, from my education in Vietnam, but I had a strong accent that people here could not understand at first. We moved into a small home at the very edge of the city, and we had very little to begin a new life. My first experience with a settlement counsellor hurt my pride and embarrassed me: the feeling of being a burden, of lost identity.

My husband got a job a week after we arrived here. When my daughter was three months old, I also went to work with my husband in a factory that made noodles. In 1979 I had to change my job three times to meet the needs of my children. Taking care of my children, going to school, and working night shift made me ill.

I started to write poems, stories of my journey in my notebooks. I would also sing to my children. That made me feel better. Later I burned my notebooks because I had written those poems and stories for me. I did not want others to be sad with my sorrow.

In 2003 my family opened the Pacific Café Cooking School on 97th Street. It is a small restaurant where I run my catering business and cooking classes. I worked very hard to create a garden at the front of this café, beside the sidewalk. I wanted to make something small and pleasing in the middle of the city. I created a sculpture of two tall golden birds, like storks, standing beside a chess set. This sculpture began with the memory of my grandfather, playing chess or reciting poetry, and drinking tea with his elderly friends, in Vietnam.

Golden birds have a special meaning in our culture. They are a symbol of respect for elders, as well as a mother's care for her children. I created the birds from papier mâché and metal clothes hangers, with steel rods for their legs on the cement base. I added two panels with a carved figure of a woman with her hands together as if she is praying or meditating. I think of her as reaching out to the world with spiritual energy.

Some bystanders took a look at my garden, with its sculptures, but it was not appreciated by others in the middle of a district where many troubled, angry, and addicted people live. At night whole plants and flowers would be dug out, and they would disappear. They left black holes in the flower beds, as well as holes in my heart. My husband suggested that I not put so much energy into this garden, but I have not given up my effort to put beautiful things in this area. Another day a man had a fight with his girlfriend, and he ran across the street, grabbing and ripping out the plants. Later, one of the golden birds was pulled out and the bird's neck snapped.

It took me a couple of months to fix the birds. I let them fly high and land on the rooftop of my building. Many people see them up there as they drive by. One reporter from the *Boyle-McCauley News* wrote a story about them.

I brought the golden birds and the chess set to my first art exhibit at Nina Haggerty Gallery this spring. Our show was called *One Heart, One Voice*. Art brings me an uplifting feeling, and it helps us to understand one another.

Nhan Thi Lu hopes to devote more time to art and writing in the years ahead. Right now she assists newcomers to Alberta through her work with the Multicultural Health Brokers Cooperative. A sculptor, she is also well-known in the city for her Southeast Asian cooking classes and for the delicious food prepared in her catering business. Every three months she prepares and edits the *Vietnamese English Lifestyle Magazine*, a bilingual publication about good health and community life. She and her husband, Tho, and their children, Dacvinh and Robbin, live in Edmonton.

SABAH TAHIR
Harmony

POETIC EDITING BY SHIRLEY SERVISS

SANGMOK LEE

Together, we set our hearts in free
  words
We sew our souls in the beauty of
  colours
Together we live in a melody
We light a candle to shine forever
You might come by to light your candle
  too
From our corner the light embarks from
every candle

Together, we pass
the deep blue of the Pacific Ocean
the rainbow over Ararat Mountain
the freedom of Vietnam's spring rain
the whiff of a wild Spanish rose
the wonder of Kurdistan's pomegranate
the cheer of the prayer mothers as they break war's moment

the smile of an African girl as she sings, overcoming her wounds
the immortality of the Great Wall of China
the flowers of Korea, waving beneath the blue sky and free birds
the maternal strength of the Montenegro bridge
Together, we travel farther than beauty
You bring me your candle to shine in my darkest night
The night I waved goodbye to my childhood
to my little town, Koya, to my mother
to a little house shining under the sun.
You bring me friendship
Together, we find the gift to speak with the wind
we find a way to live in one moment of the future
we embrace the unborn child
we end the fire of never-ending war
Together, we write the most beautiful poem
anyone has ever written
We draw a view in colours
no one else has created
Together, we are a rising tree
bending with peace in all seasons
Together, we are one single world full of colours
the colour of pomegranate
of the deep ocean
of the wild red rose
of the blue sky
of Ararat Mountain
of the sunrise
of the sunset
the colour of your smile
the colour of free people.
Together, we are a little house full of peace
We are never alone

Sabah Tahir began to write at a young age. Born in the small town of Koya, in the Kurdish region of northern Iraq, she submitted a poem to a well-known magazine, the *New Intellectual*, at the age of fifteen. Her poem was published. "As I remember it was about the hard life of women in our country," she recalls. "Since then I have tried to use my words, and my writing, to bring a better life to the women of Kurdistan and the world." She and her husband, the poet Jalal Barzanji, arrived in Alberta in 1998 as refugees, along with their three children, Ewar, Niga, and Jwamer. "We have lived happily in Edmonton since then," she says. "I will never quit writing no matter how many challenges I face." She assists newcomers to the city through her work with the Multicultural Health Brokers Cooperative.

NUNG JAI PARK
Grafted Apple Trees

TRANSLATED FROM KOREAN BY MIEUN KWAK

In my backyard there are two apple trees. They have grown into big trees as if telling the history of my family's immigration. I remember that it was twenty years ago when my family bought this house. It was just spring when we moved into our new home. This was our second move in Canada. I bought and planted two little apple trees in the yard, which have transformed into real apple trees producing lots of fruit. When I look at the apple trees through a window, I realize the passage of our long years as immigrants since we settled in Canada.

Edmonton, located at the entrance to the Arctic, is covered with green colours when its long winter passes and spring finally comes. It is the time when people get busy with raking piles of leaves from the previous year and with caring for the old lawn. People do the gardening and trim off unruly tree branches. Although I only have a small garden plot,

I plant a wide variety of vegetables like lettuce, spinach, leaf beets, and crown daisies, which I harvest in the summer.

Green sprouts grow through the soil and appear on the surface; bare trees start to look green, holding more water and new buds. I am amazed by the creator of the universe for the world's wonder and greatness. Looking at my apple trees, I had the idea that I could make my trees produce good quality apples if I grafted them with some branches of other good apple trees. Later I forgot to do it. However, I hear many other people saying that grafted fruit trees bear better quality fruit and bloom with more beautiful flowers.

Some time ago I planted roses in my garden. Wild roses grew the following year, and then I realized that I had planted grafted roses. Grafting roses to wild roses' roots creates new breeds that can flourish anywhere and give beautiful flowers. Grafting is a way of creating a new entity by cutting off a branch and inserting this scion into the stock of another plant. Grafting is meant for improvement, just like hybridization is used to improve an animal breed.

Edmonton has a cold and long winter. For that reason fruit doesn't taste good and flowers don't bear fragrance. Many households have apple trees but those trees don't produce good quality apples. People most likely harvest crab apples to make apple jam or wine. Some crab apples are fed to livestock. Not long ago good apple trees were introduced in Edmonton. They withstand cold weather better and produce good quality fruit.

Two years ago, I got some branches of my neighbour's good apple trees and grafted them to my apple trees. Some of them died but some survived. The grafted branches bloomed this year like other branches usually do. It was marvelous for me to see them blooming. Successful grafting requires careful work. There are also several conditions to keep in mind. For grafting, the same size of branches should be used and they must fit exactly. The grafted parts have to be fixed hard. This is to prevent them moving even when it is windy. I learned these lessons through my experience. I had tried grafting and a year later I found some branches had died.

My grafted tree survived the hardship, and it finally produced flourishing green leaves and beautifully blooming flowers. It was such a rewarding experience. I can't wait to see my apples this fall. Once they turn red, they will be handsome and tasty.

I immigrated to Canada, a county of big and wide lands. Remembering those early years, I feel that the immigration experience is like grafting. A small branch of Korea is grafted into a large stock of Canada. Like my grafted apple trees in the backyard, I had to work hard to adapt to a new environment and advance my skills.

Looking back to Korean history, my homeland has experienced many invasions from neighbouring countries because of its geographical location. Whenever the nation faced difficulties, Koreans stood together. While fighting against obstacles, Koreans put so much effort into developing and advancing its unique culture. Famous for good manners and politeness, Korea is known as "the country of courteous people in the East." Koreans are also well-known for being diligent and talented, as well. We are a very blessed people. Even after I moved to Canada, I kept my identity and my cultural heritage as a Korean. I believe that I contribute to Canada by bringing my cultural background and its qualities to Canadian society. This is the cultural gateway; I introduce Korea and our culture not only to Canada but also to other parts of the world.

My grafted apple trees look stronger and bloom beautiful flowers as if to show off their advancement. They remind me of Korean immigrants in Canada, and I think there is nothing wrong with seeing these similarities. I would like to suggest that the Korean government give more support to its own immigrants so that they can adapt themselves to a new environment, and then advance their lives, while combining their cultural heritage and the new qualities acquired in new country. I also suggest that the Korean government encourage emigration to other countries. Korean emigration will introduce Korean culture to the world, and we will contribute our skills where they are needed.

Nung Jai Park was born in South Korea and immigrated to Canada in 1973. He started writing in 2000 and continues his writing career by actively engaging himself in Korean literary circles.

Nung Jai has received numerous awards both inside and outside Korea. He was twice awarded the New Essay Writer of the Year in 2001 by the Korean Expatriate Literature Society and in 2007 by the Overseas Korean Foundation. He was also awarded Overseas Writer of the Year in 2001 by *Mirae Munhak*, a Korean quarterly magazine.

Nung Jai published an essay collection titled *Canadian Spring* in 2007. He is a member of the Korean Writers Association and a contributing member of *Sunsu Munkak*, a well-known monthly literary magazine in Korea. He is the president of the branch office of *Mirae Munhak* in Edmonton. He also serves as a president of the Korean Literary Club of Edmonton.

BRIAN BRENNAN
Leaving Dublin

I used to have a ready-made answer—bit of a pat one, really—when asked why I left Ireland in 1966 to come to Canada: Because I had seen the future and didn't like it. Because I worked for the civil service in Dublin, and hated every boring minute of it. Because I shared an office with a man in his sixties whose job it was to sign the letters I was responsible for drafting. If the best I could aspire to after forty years on the job was a move across the room to sign letters drafted by some twentyish junior executive officer, then it seemed to me I should be doing something else with my life.

I still believe this was a valid rationale for leaving, although it wasn't my only reason. If pressed, I might have advanced other, more high-minded reasons for leaving Ireland: state censorship, hidebound provincialism, repressive Church authority, treatment of women as second-class citizens, too many shops selling souvenir leprechauns made of bog oak. Okay, that last one might be a bit of a stretch. But escape from the civil service was undoubtedly my most compelling reason for leaving. The civil service was stultifying. The civil service was soul-destroying. There were some interesting opportunities to be found in the Parliamentary secretariat and the diplomatic corps, but those jobs were only available if you could first suffer through years of mindless paper shuffling in one of the less exciting branches of the civil service. I couldn't do that. No sooner had I landed in the Office of the Revenue Commissioners, Customs and Excise Division, Dublin Castle, than I wanted out.

If I had been older and wiser, I might have realized—like the novelist Flann O'Brien and the playwright Hugh Leonard—that in this slough of sloth I had the perfect pad for launching a career as a writer. But at age twenty-three I just wanted to get away from a job defined by tea breaks, *Irish Times* crossword puzzles, and earnest debates about the ambiguities of the Irish customs regulations. Should beach balls be classified as toys or sporting goods? Should linoleum be classified as a floor covering or a petroleum by-product? My job was to make rulings on such weighty matters, seek affirmation from my principal officer, have my clerical assistant fill in the blanks in the appropriate form letters, and then submit the letters to my higher executive officer—the man in his sixties —for signature. The whole enterprise was labour intensive to the point of wastefulness. But then, this was the Irish civil service. All the clichés were true.

Why Canada? My friend and also a former civil servant Michael Murphy used to initiate this little dialogue whenever our restless feelings got the better of us:

> *Let's go to South Africa, Brennan.*
> *It's got apartheid there.*
> *How about the States, then?*
> *No, they send you to Vietnam.*
> *How about Australia?*
> *Too far away. Besides, I hear they don't have a lot of women down there.*
> *How about Canada?*
> *That might be a possibility. We should look into it.*

Canada, in fact, was the only option. Canada was eager to attract immigrants, especially educated white immigrants like Murph and me. The federal government would fly you to the Canadian destination of your choice and cover the airfare with an interest-free loan that didn't have to be paid back for three years. It was an offer I could not refuse. Neither could Murph. He had already left the civil service job that his father had encouraged him to take after secondary school and gone to work for Jacobs Biscuits as a work-study officer. But he wasn't any happier there than he had been in the service.

Murph and I had been friends for five years when we decided to emigrate. We met at a civil service Christmas dance in Dublin where we both had our eyes on the same girl. Murph, ever the dashing Corkman, stole her attention with his captivating line of blarney. We became firm friends shortly afterwards. We were part of a group of Corkmen that included Murph's older brother, Mahon, and a civil servant named Denis O'Leary who worked in foreign affairs and—far as I could tell—had no restless feelings like those harboured by Murph and me. I qualified for membership on the strength of having spent my last year of high school in Cork, and being able to sing all the verses and choruses of such popular Cork anthems as "The Holy Ground" ("Fine girl, you are"), "The Boul' Thady Quill," and the ever-popular "Banks Of My Own Lovely Lee."

As a group, we did everything together. We spent summer weekends camping beside the beach at Brittas Bay in County Wicklow. Other weekends we spent partying, drinking, attending rugby club dances, and chatting up girls. My Corkonian comrades had been friends since schooldays, so I felt privileged to be admitted to their ranks. I had lost touch with most of my Dublin school pals after moving to Cork and felt the need to belong to a group. These gregarious Corkmen were my salvation. We learned the songs of The Beatles and the Clancy Brothers, taught ourselves how to play guitar, sang in pubs, discussed the novels of Saul Bellow and Albert Camus, attended premieres of plays by Samuel Beckett and Harold Pinter, read *The Economist* and *New Statesman,* vacationed in a cabin cruiser on the River Shannon, and climbed the Sugar Loaf Mountain.

Girls entered our lives from time to time. But girls had to understand that friendship with one of our group meant friendship with all of us—unofficial membership in our circle. Our commitment to one another was such that no girl could ever expect to do what Yoko Ono later did to The Beatles. That's not to say, of course, that some of us didn't have serious relationships. I, for example, was briefly engaged to a bank clerk whom I met during a seaside camping vacation in County Kerry. The romance ended with the summer. Then Denis O'Leary became the first in the group to marry. He fell for the daughter of a Swedish doctor when he was posted to Stockholm as a junior diplomat. Denis's wife, Suzanne, said later that when he brought her over to Ireland for the first time, he told her the other five members of our group would be at the airport to "check her out." I can well believe it. Under the circumstances, it's a wonder that any self-respecting young woman would have anything to do with this chauvinistic club of bachelors.

When Murph and I embarked for Canada, we did what no girl had ever succeeded in doing. We broke up this group of male buddies, this circle of Corkonian comradeship, once and for all. That was not our intention, of course. We just wanted to set out on an adventure across the ocean. Instead of backpacking around Europe as some of our friends were doing, we would wander around Canada for a year. But when we dined for the last time at the Lamb Doyle's restaurant in the Dublin Mountains, and then sang choruses of "Whispering Hope" around the piano for Murph's mother, we must have sensed that things would never be the same again.

Never again would we spend our Sunday afternoons at the Murphy home playing chess, trying to crack the *Observer* crossword puzzle, learning the words of the new Bob Dylan release, and applauding Mahon's clumsy efforts to master the Pete Seeger style of frailing banjo. Never again would we talk about buying a stone cottage as a summer retreat in the Wicklow hills. Never again would we gatecrash girls' parties with impunity, defending our actions on grounds that men with guitars should never be turned away. Never again would we return to the state of innocence that we shared as single Irish men in our early twenties. For innocent we truly were, unwise in the ways of the world, possessed of a naïve faith in our abilities to succeed at whatever we turned our hands to. We had been protected from the harsh realities of life by caring, supportive parents, who sacrificed much to keep us in school, give us hot dinners and good clothes, and allow us as much time as we needed before giving us wings to fly. So even if we believed we could make it on our own—and some of us had actually taken a step in this direction by moving into apartments where we paid our own gas bills—the fact is we were still essentially unprepared to deal with the kinds of economic and other problems our parents had faced during the 1930s and 1940s.

Murph and I arrived in Vancouver on Remembrance Day, November 11, 1966. Such a date you never forget. We chose Vancouver partly because it was the farthest distance from Dublin we could go on our subsidized Aer Lingus flight, and partly because the climate was similar to what we were used to. I had enough money to live on for about a month, no job, and no immediate prospects. But I was not worried. The man at the Canadian embassy in Dublin had assured me I would have no difficulty finding work in Canada. He had an ulterior motive, of course. Though I didn't know it at the time, the Lester Pearson government was actively encouraging immigration during the 1960s because it believed that immigrants of a certain kind—young, well educated, employable, and fluent in English or French—would contribute to the national objectives of maintaining a high rate of population and economic growth. All Murph and I had to do was show the man our college diplomas and we were eligible for assisted passage.

Though my background as an Irish civil servant qualified me for nothing advertised on the bulletin boards at the Canada Employment office, I felt confident there was a job waiting for me somewhere. In fact, I was so convinced of my ability to succeed that I walked into the office of CKNW Radio—the top-rated AM station in Vancouver—and asked to be a talk-show host or news announcer. Such hubris. It never occurred to me that my lack of radio experience, not to mention my Dublin accent, might be a hindrance. I had known a guy in Dublin who landed a job as newsreader with Radio-Telefís Éireann without any announcing experience. Why couldn't I do the same in Canada? The personnel man at CKNW, to his credit, didn't laugh me out of his office. I bet he dined out on the story for years afterwards.

Within a few weeks, though, I did have a job. I had applied to various finance companies and banks where the managers were eager to interview me but never actually offered me anything. I'm sure they only wanted to listen to my accent. Then I walked into the offices of Ross and Kerr Customs Brokers on Pender Street. It was lunchtime. Mr. Kerr interviewed me as he munched on his apple and bologna sandwich, and then he told me the job was mine. I would be doing the paperwork for goods imported and checked into bonded warehouses pending payment of customs duty. Not very exciting but money in the bank until something better came along.

Murph, too, landed a job about this time—as a work-study specialist for a company manufacturing steam pressure gauges for ships' boilers. He got the job after we sang Irish songs at a Grey Cup party attended by the company president. The president took a liking to Murph and offered him the job.

At this point, Murph and I were staying with the McCarron family in New Westminster. They were generous Roman Catholics who took us in after learning we had recently arrived from Ireland. A colleague at Dublin Castle had given me the name of an Irish nun, Sister Josephine, living at a New Westminster convent. As soon as I contacted her, she put the wheels in motion to find accommodation for us. The McCarrons already had four grown children of their own, all still living at home. But still they found room to accommodate two more.

It was through Mr. McCarron that I first came to know Shay Duffin, a Dublin-born singer and actor who gave me the opportunity to make my living as a performer. I had made some attempts to break into the business while living in Dublin but never got much beyond playing the occasional pub gig or variety show. Duffin made it possible for me to realize a long-cherished dream of playing music full time.

Duffin had been living in Canada for about ten years when I first met him in early 1967. He worked as an upholsterer during the day and moonlighted as a tenor singing Irish ballads at hotel banquets. When he found out I played piano, he asked me to become his regular accompanist. Murph and I continued to perform together at private parties but that was mainly for fun. With Duffin I was able to turn a hobby into an occupation.

Our first regular gig was a weekly Sunday-brunch performance at

Sambo's Pancake House in Burnaby. Initially, the place was called Little Black Sambo's, but political correctness soon changed that. We performed a mixture of Irish and easy-listening pop, from "Danny Boy" to "The Sound Of Music." Duffin did most of the singing. I had my moment of glory when he took a break and I got to do a solo spot on the piano: "Lara's Theme" and "A Walk In The Black Forest." It was technically undemanding schlock, but I was in show business. Well almost.

We still kept our day jobs. The performing kept us fairly busy, with one-nighters at golf clubs and trade shows augmenting the Sambo's gig. But there wasn't enough money in the music to warrant going full time. Not in Vancouver, at any rate.

The leap into full-time performing came in June 1967. An impresario named Fran Dowie came to see us at Sambo's and booked us into a vaudeville show he was coordinating for that summer in Dawson City, Yukon. Duffin and I had an Irish stage act put together by then. We called ourselves The Dublin Rogues, wore tweed caps and green corduroy pants, and had an LP, *Off To Dublin In The Green*, recorded for RCA. The logical next step was to quit our day jobs, call ourselves full-time performers, and hit the road.

The Dawson engagement paid less than musicians' union scale, but I managed to save more than $3,000 that summer. I worked during the day in the gold room of the Canadian Imperial Bank Of Commerce, telling visitors about sluice boxes and advising them where to go panning for gold. At night, after the two-hour Gaslight Follies show at the Palace Grand Theatre, Duffin and I entertained in the bar at the Westminster Hotel. It was far from the lights of Vegas, where we really wanted to be, but it was a step along the way.

At the end of the summer, we returned to Vancouver. I resumed work at Ross and Kerr. A month later, I quit again. "Why don't we see if we can make it in Toronto?" Duffin had asked. Why not indeed? He had a wife and four children. I was single. I had a lot less to risk.

Initially, we stayed at the Ford Hotel. When Duffin's money ran out, we moved to the YMCA. After two months in Toronto we were still waiting for our big break. We signed with the Moxie Whitney talent agency and auditioned for work with the Holiday Inn chain. We toured briefly with the Abbey Tavern Singers, who fired us after two concert dates. The Singers didn't like our parody versions of the maudlin Irish songs they sang straight. Then came our much-needed break. We auditioned for a hotel owner from Northern Ontario. He liked what he heard and booked us into the lounge of his Sudbury hotel for two weeks, for three hundred dollars each per week plus free accommodation and meals. From there, we would go to Sault Ste. Marie, Timmins, Niagara Falls, and Halifax. Ten whole weeks of uninterrupted work. I was thrilled. *Ed Sullivan Show*, watch out.

I spent eight months on the road with Duffin. For a while it was fun. The nightclub audiences were receptive, especially in Nova Scotia. At Halifax's Black Knight Lounge, and Wong's Restaurant in Antigonish, we appeared between the engagements of such wandering minstrels as the kilted John Allan Cameron and the guitar-strumming Celts. The audiences came to listen, and Duffin and I performed as if we were in concert. We did stage-Irish comedy, parodies, and traditional songs at the piano. The music industry, for the sake of easy branding, pigeonholed us with the folk acts of the period. But in our shiny black suits and bow ties (we dispensed with the caps and green corduroy pants after Dawson) we owed more to the conventions of the Vegas revue than to the down-home musical traditions of Nova Scotia.

Our career in the music business never produced a hit recording, though Duffin and I did get some radio play with our cover version of "Off to Dublin In The Green." It was an old IRA marching song that had become popular in Canada on the strength of a beer commercial for Carling Black Label. Our version of the song was good enough to land us a recording contract with RCA in early 1967, and the opportunity to do a second album after the first one sold well. We also got some airplay from a comedy song about our charismatic prime minister, "Pierre the Kissing PM." But because we put as much emphasis on our comedy as on our songs, and had little to offer in the way of creative musical achievement, we were never destined to be anything more than a marginal entry in the history of Canadian popular music.

By the spring of 1968, Duffin and I had run our course. Although we made concert appearances with such celebrities as Tommy Hunter and Anne Murray, it didn't look like we were ever going to break out of the

Canadian nightclub scene. Vegas had never beckoned, the call from Ed Sullivan had never come, and I was getting bored. Duffin was eager to move on to the next stage of his career, performing a one-man theatrical show on the life of Irish playwright Brendan Behan. I was anxious to get off the road. I had done my musical thing and wanted to spend more time with Zelda. I met her in February 1968 when I was playing in Halifax, and romance soon blossomed.

Zelda and I settled first in Vancouver, where Murph was still living but about to embark on a new overseas adventure, as a volunteer teacher in Zambia. Zelda worked as an insurance clerk while I took journalism courses at Vancouver City College. Four years later, we were living in Prince George. I worked as a city-hall reporter with the daily *Citizen* and freelanced stories to the *Vancouver Province*. My goal was to eventually land a full-time job at the *Province,* but fate intervened in the form of a job offer from the *Calgary Herald.* The year was 1974. "Sure, let's go to Calgary for a year," I said to Zelda. "Then we can move back to Vancouver."

We never went back to Vancouver. My year in Calgary became like my year in Canada—the year I had told my mother in 1966 that I would spend here before returning to Ireland. After a few months in Canada, I knew I would never go back to Dublin. After a few months in Calgary, I knew I had found my true home. Canada had given me the opportunity to fulfil my boyhood dream of becoming a professional musician. Calgary gave me the opportunity to set down roots, work full time as a journalist, and make a good life with my Canadian wife and daughter. Calgary was, and remains for me, a city where the future has always promised nothing but brightness.

Brian Brennan worked as a staff writer at the *Calgary Herald* for twenty-five years. He resigned in 1999 to write books about the colourful personalities and social history of western Canada. His seven titles include the best-selling *Scoundrels and Scallywags: Characters from Alberta's Past* and *How the West was Written,* the first in-depth biography of renowned prairie social historian James H. Gray. His latest biography, *The Good Steward: The Ernest C. Manning Story,* appeared in 2008. Brennan still plays the piano when asked.

MIEKE ALEXANDER
Atlantic Crossing

SHABNAM SUKHDEV

We are on the ship, and there is no turning back. My family is getting smaller and smaller, and tears are streaming down my face.

The year is 1967. All of us—my mam, brothers, sisters, and cousins—had come to the city of Rotterdam. We had plenty of time to say goodbye in the hall of the Holland America line before boarding. We had finished our last cup of coffee together. Patricia, our two-year-old, was having fun with her cousins, until the time came to board the *Maasdam,* the last emigrant ship to leave from this dock.

This is the day we had planned for so long, talked about and looked forward to. Now it is here. I can't seem to swallow the lump in my throat. I am sad, scared, excited. My emotions are all over the place. I stand at the railing with Vince, my husband, and our little two-year-old in my arms. We are waving to our disappearing family.

Looking at my husband, my eyes are asking: What have we done, we are taking our little girl away from all her family? I am frightened.

He squeezes my hand and says: "We will be alright, you'll see." The city is gone; the countryside is gliding by.

My mind goes back to how this all came about.

What made us come to this moment, to this decision to leave all that is familiar and good and to go to something completely unknown and new?

It had all started a few years before, talking about going to Canada, reading about it, making numerous visits to the Canadian embassy in The Hague, and believing in this exciting, new adventure.

We were just two adults then, but now we are three. The full impact of the decision hits me smack in my heart.

Slowly I move away from the railing, dry my tears, take a deep breath, and manage to smile. He said we would be okay. I have to believe that.

It is time to find our cabin and get to know the layout of this big ship. I can feel the waves now; we are in the North Sea. More people going to Canada will be picked up. Our first stop is LeHavre, France, from there to Southampton, England, and Cork, Ireland, before crossing the Atlantic Ocean to arrive in Halifax, in Canada.

It does not take us long to find all the important things necessary for our ten-day stay on the ship. We find the dining room, store, deck chairs, even a daycare, where you can leave your little one, if you want to watch a movie or read in the library. We have our lifeboat drill. Soon we settle in for the long crossing.

It is March and storms in the Atlantic Ocean are quite frequent at this time of the year. Seasickness hits Vince full force, and he spends most of his time moaning on a deck chair or lying on his bed in the cabin. I look after Patricia and make the best of things. The weather is very bad and lots of passengers are seasick. Ropes are wound around stairways for people to hang on to, the front and aft decks are off limits, and tablecloths are made wet so the dishes do not slide all over the place.

It is quite an art to feed our two-year-old, and ourselves, and poor Vince is getting sicker and sicker.

In the daycare I am told to stay with Patricia. Playpens, high chairs, and cribs are fastened to the floor; anything else just does the sliding dance. One minute the kids all slide to one end of the room, and with a big heave of the next wave, they all slide on their little bums back again.

The storm never lets up until the day, when we see the coastline of Nova Scotia. The pilot comes on board and we enter the Halifax Harbour.

My heart jumps and the excitement of the unknown starts to creep back into my soul.

All of us are herded into Pier 21, the famous gateway to Canada, where we spend the rest of the day going through all kinds of paperwork and formalities before walking into the country as new landed emigrants. Goodbye sea-legs, goodbye seasickness. We have arrived and are ready to become part of this wonderful land.

Before stepping on the train, to travel to our final destination, Edmonton, Alberta, we collect our large wooden trunk. It contains our possessions and mementoes connecting us with the life and the family we have left behind. We sit on the on the train for four days to go from Halifax to Edmonton with a five-hour stopover in Montreal. There seems to be no end to the countryside, the villages and the forest we are travelling through. Sometimes the train stops for hours as crews clear snow from the tracks. The beds we sleep on at night are converted back to seats in the morning so we can enjoy the views outside. It is midnight when we arrive at the station in Edmonton. A friendly taxi driver takes us to a small motel close to the City Centre Airport. We are ready to sleep for the first night in our new city.

Many years later . . .

We still live in Edmonton. An old trunk adorns our home, with the stickers from the Holland America Line still visible on the outside. The dishes we so carefully packed and brought with us are all gone, but the treasures from back home are still with us. Our family has grown from one to three daughters, all grown up now with children of their own. I think back many times of that great adventure we undertook so many years ago to come to this city we call home.

Mieke Alexander was born in Delft in the Netherlands on January 13, 1944. She was the second youngest in a family of eight children. She and her husband and two-year-old daughter arrived in Canada on the last immigrant ship to dock at Pier 21 in Halifax in March 1967. Mieke lives in Edmonton and enjoys writing and storytelling.

YI LI
Swimming Home

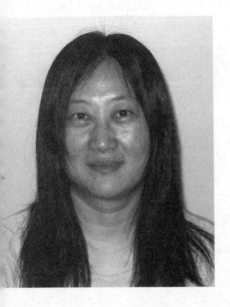

I first heard about the story of Fraser River Chinook salmon in British Columbia while on a guided canoe tour in the Canadian Rockies. It was a cold and misty morning in early June 1998. I had just emigrated from Shanghai, China, to join my husband, Guoji, in Jasper, Alberta, for three months. I still wore my winter jacket while the rest of the walkers in the tour group wore their spring sweaters. As we watched birds, moose, and eagles, one of us brought up the topic of the salmon, which the guide explained briefly to us.

Later that day, on a rafting tour along the Fraser River, the same guide showed us the spawning grounds of those Chinook salmon. I was not particularly impressed until he led us to the Rearguard Falls, where the Chinook salmon had to jump upstream in order to reach their home stream to spawn. There were no salmon to be seen at that time of year, and we were a little disappointed. However, the guide told us that the best time to come and watch those spectacular salmon is at the end of August and in early September.

A year later I was finally able to go back and watch those Chinook salmon. On August 25, 1999, just before I returned to Edmonton to begin my second year of my master's program at the University of Alberta, Guoji took a day off from his work and drove me to Valemount in British Columbia.

Despite the sunshine that afternoon, we could not see the peak of Mount Robson, the highest mountain in the Canadian Rockies. At the information centre, the clerk showed us, on a map, two spots where we could observe the Chinook salmon. We headed to the Rearguard Falls first. We stood there waiting for something to happen. Just as we were about to give up, Guoji exclaimed, "Look, there's a salmon jumping!" I stared at the falls but saw nothing. Several minutes later, I watched a salmon jump out of the white water and disappear within seconds. I wondered whether it had succeeded in such rapid torrents.

After quite a while, I spotted three more salmon jumping out of the white water. I could not tell whether it was the same salmon or not as I was observing from quite a distance. But from the bottom of my heart I wished these salmon would overcome this last obstacle on their long journey home.

On the way to our second observation point in Valemount, I became silent, thinking about those Chinook salmon. Hatched in fresh water, they spent part of their life in the ocean, and now they were coming home to spawn, after which they would all die. Why would they undertake such an extensive migration to reach their home streams after years of residence in the ocean?

My thoughts were interrupted by Guoji's voice. "Here we are! The Swift Creek," he announced. I jumped out of the car and walked quickly towards the creek. I was excited to see four or five large salmon swimming together in slow-moving water along the bank. The water was so clear that I could see them right in front of my eyes. They varied in size, from five to thirteen kilograms. It took them quite a while to swim even a short distance because they were moving upstream. One smaller salmon was rushed downstream but very soon turned around and resumed its journey against the water flow.

I sat down to watch the Chinook salmon closely while Guoji walked farther and farther upstream along the bank. I was still lost in my thoughts when he came back. He asked me when I wanted to leave. I was happy to do so once I had taken pictures of those wonderful creatures.

I did not think about the salmon story until January 2000 when I took a narrative inquiry course at the University of Alberta. I was struggling to find a metaphor to understand the journey my research participants and many other overseas Chinese students took and would continue to take. They were born and brought up in China, finished high school or university there, and came overseas to study for at least one university degree. Some would return to their homeland on completion of their studies while others would choose to stay and make a new home in Canada. What would make them want to stay overseas? What would make them want to go back home? What is home?

At that time I intended to finish my graduate studies as soon as possible and go back to Shanghai, my home. I felt I didn't have a home in Canada. It was only due to educational opportunities here that I was separated from my loved ones. I studied in Edmonton while Guoji worked in Jasper and our daughter, Yan-Yan, lived with my parents-in-law in Shanghai. Although I visited Yan-Yan in between terms, I missed her terribly. I finally decided to bring her to Edmonton in May 2000. She was three months away from her fourth birthday.

When my parents flew in from Shanghai to celebrate my master's degree in August 2001, Guoji took a week off and we went to the Canadian Rockies for a holiday. I wanted to show my parents those spectacular salmon. We arrived at the Swift Creek on August 22. Both Yan-Yan and my parents were fascinated by this natural phenomenon as it was the first time they had seen with their own eyes how the salmon were swimming upstream. I was struck by the number of salmon in the creek and wondered if we could see more of them at the Rearguard Falls. We watched more salmon jump out of the white water within shorter intervals. Every time we spotted one, we would clap our hands and cheer it on. "Watching the salmon run will certainly be the highlight of our trip to Canada," my father concluded as we headed back to Jasper.

After that trip, my family decided to begin a tradition of visiting the salmon—my salmon, Guoji and Yan-Yan often reminded me—every time we go to the Canadian Rockies in August. We know that these salmon are going home, and we want to cheer them on.

We were not able to visit the salmon again for two years. I had been busy with my doctoral research about the experiences of home and homelessness among international students from China. Guoji had taken a year off from his work in Jasper so that he could stay with us and go to school in Edmonton. Yan-Yan had started kindergarten.

"Mom, you are going to see lots of them this time," Yan-Yan told me on our way to Calgary. It was August 28, 2003. There was obvious excitement in her voice. Guoji had already taken her to see those salmon two weeks before because I was too busy working.

Two days later, we left Jasper to see the salmon run. It was a bright sunny morning with a beautiful, clear, blue sky. We had not planned to stop along the way, but we changed our mind the moment we saw the snow-covered top of Mount Robson in the distance. This was the first time in all these mountain trips during the previous five years that she did not hide herself away from us behind a veil of clouds. A few minutes later, Guoji, Yan-Yan, and I were on the hiking trail along the Mount Robson River. We stopped here and there to look up at the magnificent mountain.

When we arrived at the Rearguard Falls, it was already 2:45 PM. As I focused my attention on the two usual spots where the salmon would jump upstream, I noticed that there seemed to be more rocks in the white water this year; this was probably due to the lower water level. After waiting for ten minutes or so, I spotted one salmon jump out of the white water. It disappeared seconds later. I continued to wait, hoping it would make a second attempt. But Yan-Yan urged me to leave to look in a different place. She was running up and down the stone stairs, complaining that she hadn't seen one salmon yet this time.

Guoji turned to me with a question. "There are far fewer salmon now than two weeks ago. How long do you want to stay here and watch them?"

I could stay here forever, I thought to myself. I knew they were coming back to the river that they left. Even though it was a bad year with very dry weather and fewer salmon would make it, they were coming home. And I wanted to watch them. I did not want to leave so I answered, "Maybe until both you and Yan-Yan see one salmon."

Yan-Yan stopped running around and stood beside Guoji and me to watch the falls. "Is this just one salmon?" she asked. Hearing no response from us, she continued, "Maybe that's the only one, but it can't make it over the falls. Mom, I think I know a reason. Maybe it doesn't like the water . . . Oh, Mom! I see one!"

Yes, indeed, we saw one big salmon jump out of the white water, but it slid back right downstream under the water and disappeared. Oh, no, we all sighed, feeling sorry that it did not succeed.

"Salmon, salmon, hurry up! Let us see you jump!" Yan-Yan started chanting in Chinese. "Oh, Mom, it rhymes!" she switched to English and then back to her Chinese chanting. She was trying everything she could to help the salmon go home.

"Only the strongest salmon can swim this far from the Pacific Ocean," I said, starting to walk slowly up the stairs on our way out. I turned my head several times, hoping to see one more salmon jump upstream. None did.

We arrived at the Swift Creek at four o'clock. As soon as Guoji stopped the car, I jumped out and walked quickly to the spot where I could watch the salmon most closely. I noticed the mark on a wooden stick nearby. The water level was ten centimetres lower than usual. The creek seemed narrower with a lot of pebbles on the other side. There were no salmon in sight. As I looked farther, I saw one salmon caught in shallow water among the pebbles. It twisted its tail and managed to move to the deeper water to continue its journey upstream. I cheered loudly with the other tourists.

Guoji brought the video-camera to me. He knew I would want to tape these wonderful creatures every time I visited them. This time I stopped short when I noticed that one salmon was not moving in my viewfinder. I looked up and saw another salmon lying on the pebbles, motionless. My heart sank as I spotted several more dead salmon. My video camera suddenly felt so heavy that I had to sit down and stop the videotaping. I closed my eyes for a while, trying to recover from the shock.

"Look, Mom, there are two salmon swimming towards us," Yan-Yan exclaimed. I opened my eyes and saw a larger and a smaller salmon swimming together.

"Aren't you happy that there are two alive, and not all died?" Yan-Yan tried to comfort me.

"Perhaps, this year there are fewer salmon coming home," Guoji added. "It has been so dry. With such a low water level, it is difficult for them to swim home." Obviously, neither Guoji nor Yan-Yan was prepared to see this sight, either.

With two other tourists, we followed these two salmon along the bank, moving back and forth as the salmon did in the water. We cheered when they swam upstream; we called out, "Oh, no, come back!" when they were swept downstream. It was so difficult for them to move even a short distance ahead.

"They surely need a lot of determination to go home," I said.

As we walked farther and farther upstream, we saw more and more dead salmon floating down the creek with their white bellies towards the sky.

"We should have a scarecrow in the water," Yan-Yan said when we saw a crow eating a dead salmon. Just then I saw a large salmon floating by down the stream. I could tell it was still alive, but it did not swim. It just went with the water flow. I wondered if it had used up all its energy and had given up.

When we saw a local young man walking towards us, Guoji stopped him and asked, "Why are so many salmon dead this year?"

"Oh, their spawning ground is not far from here. They all die after spawning. And it's the end of August already," he told us matter-of-factly and walked away.

"They are dead fish now, but there's going to be lots of baby salmon next year, Mom, maybe triplets or . . . I don't want to see them dead. Bye-bye!" Yan-Yan turned around and started walking back. Guoji and I followed her.

On our way home to Edmonton, Yan-Yan fell into an exhausted sleep on the back seat. Sensing that I probably needed some quiet time Guoji drove the car without saying a word.

I felt like crying but couldn't. I knew that in their death, and in what they are trying to do, lies the genesis of the next generation of salmon. I knew that it is the way, the circle of life. But it was still so hard for me to watch them struggling upstream in order to go home. I wondered what drives them to come all this way from the ocean.

One year later, on September 5, 2004, we visited the Swift Creek again when Guoji's brother flew in from New York City to have a holiday with us. The creek was very quiet and after a long while, we spotted only one dead salmon at the bottom of the creek. It was almost one metre long, lying between the pebbles with its white belly facing upward. I wondered if it was happy that it fulfilled its responsibility towards the next generation. I wondered if it ever regretted its choice of coming home instead of staying in the ocean. I wondered if it ever regretted leaving home some years earlier.

I didn't go to visit the Chinook salmon in August 2005. Instead, I flew down to San Diego, California, to visit my sister. I was exhausted trying to write the last chapter of my dissertation. I didn't want to see the salmon struggling upstream in order to go home. They know where home is. They can keep on going because they are almost there when I see them in the Rocky Mountains. They are back. They are home. And they are going to die. In a way, the salmon know what they are doing their whole lives. But unlike them, I don't always know what is next in my life. It is difficult to live in a liminal space, a threshold.

When I sat at the beach on Coronado Island near San Diego, watching white waves upon waves rush to the shore, I wondered if any of the Chinook salmon from the Fraser River would ever reach this part of the Pacific Ocean. If some did, would they prefer the warm Californian sunshine and want to stay here for the rest of their lives? Would they want to be buried here when they die? Is this homemaking in the ocean less a struggle for them than their homecoming journey upstream in the river? Or is there always a struggle no matter where their home is . . .

As my residence in Edmonton has extended into its tenth year, I have come to feel more at home here because of all the friends I have made over the years at Research Issues at the Centre for Research for Teacher Education and Development, my academic home place at the University of Alberta. Every Tuesday afternoon, the centre hosts Research Issues

Conversations for graduate students and faculty to share and refine their research projects. I appreciate their company and their ideas.

Looking at the pictures again while writing this story, I noticed for the first time that the salmon are swimming upstream in pairs or groups of three or four. While I see each salmon negotiate whether to make its home in the river or in the ocean, I imagine they, too, connect with their families and friends, making their journey home a communal one. My friends in Edmonton have taught me that home is lived within a community, and I am thankful for having learned that in my struggle to find home.

I haven't visited the salmon for the past three summers, but I often think about their going-home story. As I wonder what the journey is like for each one of them and what makes them keep going, I wonder what sustains me as an immigrant in Canada. What sustains my hope? And what am I hoping for? Do I seek a home or create one? How do I live home in my everyday life? Who would watch over me with loving and watchful eyes as I try and try again? Who would always return to cheer me on in this new place? And who will remember me in my old home?

Now I feel much less need to see the salmon. I am ready to let go of my old going-home story. The salmon story is only one of the many possible stories I can live by around home. As I complete my second year of a postdoctoral fellowship in hope research, I wonder what new stories I will be able to create as to how I might make, find, and live home as my life unfolds in a new place, Winnipeg, Manitoba, Canada. I am moving to a new home again.

Born and raised in Shanghai, China, Yi Li moved to Edmonton as a landed immigrant in September 1998 to begin graduate studies at the University of Alberta. Previously she had taught English for almost ten years in Tong Ji University and worked as an interpreter and translator at Shanghai TV Station for two years. She obtained her master of Education in June 2001 and her Ph.D. in June 2006. Her doctoral work explored Chinese international students' experiences of home and homelessness in Canada. She worked as a post-doctoral fellow in hope research at the University of Alberta and the Hope Foundation of Alberta. Her research focuses on the role of hope in newcomer students' lives as they learn English in high school. Yi Li accepted a faculty position at the University of Manitoba in 2008.

GARY GARRISON
Political Amputee

Once a week for the past six years I've entered Edmonton's maximum-security federal prison—the Max—to talk to prisoners. Many of the prisoners I visit are serving life sentences for killing somebody. I have been living in Canada since 1970, cut off from parents, siblings, friends, and my past, because my own country's government would have put me in a prison for *not* killing people.

Whenever I leave the Max, and the steel barriers clang shut behind me, I remember the razor wire that separates these prisoners from family and friends on the outside. The line between the United States and Canada is not only razor-thin; it is in many places invisible, a symbol on a map, ephemeral as a spoken word. For me, it might as well have been made of iron.

The My Lai massacre occurred on March 16, 1968. In that Vietnamese village, three American platoons raped, tortured, and maimed 504 unarmed women, children, and seniors before slaughtering them. Lt. William Calley was the only soldier convicted of anything; he was in a military prison four and a half months. He claimed he was following orders. President Richard Nixon let him off lightly. Commentators noted how effectively the war had transformed ordinary young men into ruthless predators. By that time I already knew Nixon's defence for the war was the same as the American pronunciation of the village's name: "me lie." I decided not to become another Calley.

I was already living in Toronto when I received my draft notice. My father was a Second World War vet. He phoned me, accused me of treason and cowardice, said I was an embarrassment to the family, ordered me to tell the draft board: "Sorry I'm late. I'll be right there." I refused. It was one of the few long-distance calls he made to anyone between the Depression and 1990.

For five years I couldn't return to the US without risking arrest. My mother told me that FBI agents came to visit her to frighten her into getting me back. I often woke up in the middle of the night, shaking in a cold sweat after a dream: agents would roll me out of bed, handcuff me, put a hood over my head, shove me into the back of a van, bury me in a dank prison cell back in the States.

I was working as a journalist and was halfway through a Ph.D. in English at the University of Alberta in 1975, when I learned that charges against me had been dropped on a technicality. By then I had a life in Canada, my relationship with my parents and siblings was tenuous, and I was focused on my new family and my present and future prospects in Edmonton: teaching postsecondary English, co-parenting three children, editing *Alberta Hansard* for over twenty years, writing poetry, songs, and nonfiction, and involving myself in a variety of cultural and community groups.

In July 2007 I went to the "Our Way Home Reunion" in Castlegar, BC, a gathering of Vietnam-era draft dodgers, deserters, and anti-war veterans. When I got there and had the chance to tell my story, my voice broke. I wept. I listened to men who entered the military and later discovered that it was an unjust war. I talked with a Quaker man who joined the army with a personal mission to educate soldiers about the evils of the war and turn them against their military and political bosses. I listened to 1960s icons Daniel Ellsberg and Tom Hayden, and to Holly Near, who entertained anti-war GIs with Jane Fonda in 1971.

I met a man who drove up from Kentucky with his twenty-year-old daughter. He had planned to immigrate to Canada in 1970 as I did, but fate intervened. In the draft lottery, his birthday was drawn 289th, mine thirty-ninth, guaranteeing that I would be drafted and he wouldn't. I talked to Doukhobors whose ancestors had fled Russian military service a hundred years before. I heard the local MLA talk about his own decision to dodge the draft and how he had travelled to a place where war resistance was normal, and he had finally felt able to relax and breathe freely.

I encountered two youngsters, both about twenty, who had deserted the US Army and came to Canada to avoid deployment to Iraq. I could have been any of them and they could have been me. In those young deserters I saw myself thirty-seven years ago: naïve, disillusioned, innocent, full of energy, wary of a borderline as real as a scalpel that would sever a hand.

I lost a piece of myself when I escaped from military service. After I came to Canada, I was detained at the border once; otherwise crossing has been quick and easy. When I flew to Phoenix last December to visit my mother, the immigration officer at the airport noticed the Oklahoma birthplace indicated on my Canadian passport, rubber-stamped it, smiled, and jolted me, not with a taser, but with friendly words. *Welcome home.* As I write this I realize it still is home for part of me even now.

Parts of me are like an amputated limb that aches and itches long after worms are finished with it. My infant self still rides across Arizona, California, Nevada, Colorado in the back of a white '49 Chevy sedan as my father searches for work after his own war. I am a teenager behind our mustard-yellow suburban house in Overland Park, Kansas, leaping as high as I can to catch the baseballs my dad throws over my head to test my reach. I am a twenty-one-year-old newlywed driving across the Port Huron/Sarnia bridge to Canada with my twenty-year-old wife to escape Calley-fication.

I love the Canadian Rockies and Canada, but my first book of poetry is inspired by the Grand Canyon, a place I first saw as a child. The canyon keeps calling to me as if I originated there and have to go back, but only to visit. I am free now, and I choose to draft my life here in Edmonton.

Gary Garrison is president of the Edmonton Stroll of Poets Society and writes poems for patients at the University of Alberta Hospital as a volunteer in the Artists on the Wards program. He is also a volunteer coordinator with the M2W2 program, a Mennonite Central Committee Alberta project that began in 1983 and now sponsors visits and socials at four federal prisons in the province.

Garrison is beginning a career as a spiritual director after completing training in June 2008. He is preparing three poetry manuscripts this year and expects to publish his first collection of poetry before he turns sixty in December 2008. A family oral history/memoir and a book based on his work with prisoners, volunteers, and prison staff are also in progress.

My Grandfather's Poem, My Grandmother's Dance

I grew up in Burundi, in the capital city, Bujumbura. My parents and grandparents had come to Burundi from Rwanda as refugees in the 1950s. The troubles in Rwanda did not begin with the genocide in 1994. It started before. My grandparents and parents had to leave all of their belongings, and risk everything, to travel to Burundi to save their lives.

At that time, life was very hard for them. They had nothing when they arrived in their new country, and they were very sad. My grandparents were artists. They had to reorganize their lives in a way so that they wouldn't feel this sadness every day for the rest of their lives. They searched for happiness through their art.

My grandfather, Mazina Denis, or Diyoniziyo, was a writer. He had once been a judge in Rwanda, and a vice chief, but he had escaped to Burundi with nothing but his life and his family. In his new home, when I was visiting him as a child, he would get out of bed at two or three in the morning to write, and he would wake up us children to go and get him something. He wrote a form of poetry that Rwandans call *Ibyivugo*, a long poem about the struggles of life and heroism. He chose to write about his experiences as a refugee in this way. He described how he left his country and how he loved his country. He wrote about the large house he had built for his family in Rwanda and how he missed it. This house had seventeen rooms, and tourists would come to look at it and admire it; unfortunately it was destroyed during the genocide of 1994.

I grew up with my parents and five brothers and three sisters in the same city in Burundi where my grandparents lived. We lived in a different house, but we would go to visit them at Christmas, at the New Year, and other times. We all gathered together, about sixty cousins, uncles and aunts, on these occasions. Today the members of this big family live in countries all over the world: Canada, Cameroon, Italy, South Africa, Belgium, Zambia, France, Congo, Holland, the United Kingdom, Tanzania, Uganda, and Kenya—one cousin is even in Tahiti. But back then we gathered in my grandparents' small house, the meeting place for all of us. Of course, we weren't all there at the same time.

Often, we heard my grandfather's long poem.

When I was young, I listened to this poem from the beginning to the end many times. Perhaps, fifty times altogether. It was a long poem. It might take my grandfather fifteen minutes to recite it. In our language, Kinyarwanda, this poem was called *Icyivugo cya Mazina cyo Guhunga*, which means in English, *A Poem of Mazina from Exile*. This poem explains how he and his friends escaped the Hutus who forced them to flee their country. Some of these people ended up in the bush and were killed by animals. In the poem, my grandfather would talk about the pain that brought him to Burundi, but also about his happiness to live with his beautiful second wife, my grandmother. He wrote about how he met her and how much he loved her. He wrote that he was fortunate to have his wife, his children, and his grandchildren around him in a new land.

The first time I heard the poem I was about fifteen. I didn't understand it, but the words sounded very beautiful to me. I loved the way he talked his about feelings, his actions, and how brave he was.

People would sit outside my parents' house, under the eucalyptus trees, the papaya trees, the green trees, to listen to him when he visited us. He said he remembered the first time he saw white people when he was a child in Rwanda. He called them "the big babies" because their skin was so light like an infant.

He was very tall and strong and a little strict with us, but we loved him. He was also a guitarist, with the *inanga*, a traditional instrument. Even as an older man, he would ride a bicycle. He refused to take a ride in a car. He preferred to walk instead, in traditional clothes, a proud, old man. He would tell us: "I've had a dream that I am going to die soon." When he was 105, he was hit by a truck. So everyone said: "Now, he is going to die." But he didn't! As an old man he continued to write, to paint, and to make carvings as gifts for people he liked—but his writing was the most important to him.

"Everything I write in my notebooks you will have when I die," he told us. He said his poems and stories would make us proud of him after he left the world. He locked his many notebooks in a suitcase. He hoped to carry it back to his country because he wanted to be buried in Rwanda.

Unfortunately, that didn't happen. My grandfather died in Burundi at a very old age in 1988. We were told he was 118 years old.

There is a sad reason why his writing of a lifetime was not passed on to us, or published. Something terrible happened. At the time of his funeral, someone who was working inside his house found the box, the suitcase, where he kept his notebooks, with his important life poem, and many other poems. This person was curious because the suitcase was locked. He thought there was money inside it. He took the suitcase away, and then he just disappeared.

My grandmother, and all of us, were sad because we knew that the writing was the possession that my grandfather valued the most.

Somehow at least his long poem survived. My uncle, Hassan Harbi, who is also a writer, found the suitcase at last. My grandfather's voice is still with us, too. I have two cousins, Ephrem and Georges Sebatigita, who have a tape recording of my grandfather reciting his poem. The tape is in Burundi. My dream is that I will put my hand on this tape, or the notebooks, and write down every word, and find a way to publish it here.

I moved to Canada with my husband in 1991. Why did I come here? Even in Burundi, a person does not always feel safe. The hatred that caused a genocide in Rwanda spilled into other countries. People kill each other. I was a young woman, a peaceful person, with a baby. I did not want to raise my children in a society where they were not safe.

Now I want to tell you about the courage of my widowed grandmother and her sister when they were very old.

My two grandmothers, I call them—that would be my grandmother Mukazi Pascasie and her sister, Nyirankoko Costasie—had been famous in Rwanda as dancers and singers when they were young women. They were like twins. They composed songs, and they taught children how to do the traditional dances in a special school they organized. They had even danced for the King in Rwanda when they were younger.

By the time I was a little girl, my grandmother and her sister were older women, but they still looked strong and beautiful. They were very active. I knew they were famous because so many people would come to see them. The two sisters held women's gatherings, and in 1988, they started a small humanitarian organization of eleven Rwandan women called Benimpuhwe, a word that means compassion, to help the Rwandan exiles who were coming to Burundi more and more.

Women would come to their house to sing, to recite poems, to tell stories and jokes to one another. My grandmother was well-organized with these activities, and so generous. Once she gave away all of her clothes to someone who needed them. Many years later, here in Edmonton, I went to my son's school and found pictures of Rwanda in a display window, and one picture was of my grandmother. That amazed me. Perhaps her picture arrived here before I did.

I was here in Canada in 1994 when the genocide happened in Rwanda. The massacre left 800,000 men, women, and children dead, probably many thousands more. All of the killing happened in just one hundred days, from April 6 until the middle of July. A great-grandfather of mine, Kayijuka, had known that this massacre would happen. He had predicted Rwanda would face a terrible genocide but that refugees would return to Rwanda after many years in exile. He knew what was coming. Like many, many people with family roots in Rwanda, I lost cousins and friends in the genocide.

I have only returned once from Canada to see my family in Africa, in 1995, but we did not enjoy the visit too much because it was such a sad time for us all.

Do you know what happened after the genocide?

My grandmother and her sister decided to leave Burundi and go back to Rwanda together with the Benimpuhwe women. They were very brave. They said they would never live anywhere else again, they would die there, too, in their true country. My cousins in Europe said: "Come to us." But they would not go.

Like many people, they were hungry to go home to Rwanda. It was hard for them to start life in a country with so much grief and suffering around them. They didn't know whether the dangerous times would come back. But these two grandmothers and the other women collected money and started a village in the countryside—Rilima in the Gashora district—to make a home for the people who had lost their families to the massacres, and lost their homes, too. They made small farms and handicrafts centres, and their group built 180 houses with the help of international organizations. Today, more than 1,600 people live in Rilima. That's where they stayed, too. My grandmother's sister, Nyirankoko, died there on April 18, 2008. She was ninety-four.

I am going to see my grandmother in Rwanda in December. We will have a big celebration for her 100th birthday. She uses crutches now and can no longer dance, but she is still beautiful. She teaches traditional singing to people who come to see her, and she makes baskets and necklaces and other handicrafts. Her songs and dances survived the genocide, and a new generation of Rwandans is learning them.

She says, "I don't want to die until I see Chantal again." She has only seen one of my three children.

When I came to Canada I realized how much I missed my grandparents. I said to myself: I need my grandfather's poem. I am an exile like him. When I lived near him, I thought: The poem is here. It will always be here. But then it was taken away from us.

When you move away, you lose so much, but not everything.

I brought my memories to Canada. I missed watching Rwandan dances, but my grandmother had taught them to me, so I know them. I brought my thoughts about my grandfather's poem. I had grown up in an artistic environment so I couldn't live without these things.

My husband and I moved to Montreal at first because we spoke French, as well as our own language. When my sisters-in-law moved to Edmonton with their families, I didn't want my children to be lonely without their cousins, so we moved here in 2000. It was a struggle to speak English all the time, although I had known some English before I came.

To feel better, and more at home, I tried to get involved in art and performance as soon as I came here. I joined a global choir and traditional drumming groups. I am also involved in different kinds of fundraising for African students here, because so many of them are suffering from homesickness and loneliness.

I want Canadians to understand the genocide that happened in my country. I want them to welcome Rwandans and other African refugees and feel the pain of these people, the pain that still exists in their souls. Many Canadians don't understand the life of Rwandan refugees here. The genocide is still traumatizing for these people. They were not used to this kind of violence. They remember their childhood years when their neighbours loved one another and shared their homes with strangers before the hard times came. Many people who come here to Edmonton from another country are isolated because of the bad memories and fears that still haunt them. They need our support.

My dream is to open a cultural centre in Edmonton to teach traditional dancing, songs, and drumming, and to bring Rwanda's highly developed drama to this city. We Rwandans are now around two thousand people in Alberta. We are everywhere.

Art can heal people. Music and dance and poems can take away suffering. This is the healing my grandparents experienced when they escaped from Rwanda to Burundi. They realized they were happy when they were expressing their artistic feelings. They gave me this spirit, too: the love of the drum, the dance, the song, and the poem. They gave me the strength of my family. I want to bring their happiness to Edmonton.

Chantal Hitayezu assists newcomers to Alberta through her work with the Multicultural Health Brokers Co-operative. She is a member of the 1994 Genocide Memory Keepers Association. In her free time, she is an active community volunteer and enjoys relaxing with her three children, Bozi Abdallah, Macha Abdallah, and Maya Abdallah, and her husband, Juma Abdallah. She also performs with a traditional drumming group in Edmonton.

MARY CAVILL
Missing England

In post-war England my husband and I, along with our son and daughter, lived in Rochester, Kent, the Garden of England, by the River Medway, just twenty miles from London. Our decision in 1957 to come to Edmonton, and leave behind family and friends along with our way of life, was traumatic.

I had enjoyed a happy, carefree childhood. My parents, two sisters, and grandparents played an important part of my life. My sailor grandfather was special. The sea was his life. I spent many happy times with him running barefoot in the sand and paddling in the water when the tide was in. I watched the ships sailing to and from London with their cargos from around the world. My grandfather raised and lowered the Union Jack flag daily and taught me how to salute it naval fashion. I learned how to tie knots as his large, calloused hands gently guided my small fingers around the string to be tied. I loved him dearly.

To this day I can recall the delicious smell coming from the kitchen where my grannie was cooking. She made toffee apples as a special treat and allowed us to pick pears and plums from the orchard. Grannie enjoyed having her grandchildren around but insisted on obedience.

She was a small woman always dressed in black except at Sunday church. There she wore a white blouse with her best skirt. At home she kept her knitting in the large pocket of her voluminous, white apron. She taught me to knit when I was four years old and I have enjoyed knitting ever since.

My paternal grandmother was quite different. We called her Grandma and knew we had to be on our best behaviour while visiting. She offered her cheek for a kiss before motioning us to sit down. Her sitting room was filled with large, stately inlaid pieces of furniture and the walls were covered with artifacts brought home by her two military sons during their army careers. The chairs we sat on were slippery, and our short legs could not reach the floor, making it difficult to sit still as my mother had instructed. We sat quietly, answering her questions politely, but we were relieved when we were sent outside. Here flowers surrounded us. I loved the scents, colours, and shapes of the blooms, especially carnations, but I was frightened by the geese that always chased me. I preferred to watch the ducks on a nearby pond.

I had no idea why there was no grandfather with Grandma, but learned later that he had been involved in a stocks-and-shares financial collapse. He had suffered a fatal heart attack and died in his early forties. Grandma was a midwife. Along with these responsibilities and the care of a large family, she opened a shop in the front of her house and sold fruit, vegetables, sweets, and chocolates. After her death the family learned her late husband's financial investments had recovered over the years, and she had inherited unexpected money and property.

My father was a regular soldier who, at the age of fourteen, became a cadet in the British army after his father's sudden death. Two of his older brothers were commissioned army officers, and another served in the Army Pay Corps. So, the military was the apex of their lives.

During the Great War, 1914 to 1918, Dad served in the Thirteenth Middlesex Regiment, surviving the horrors of the Battle of the Somme and Ypres. While in the trenches he was exposed to deadly chlorine gas, which destroyed his lungs. An enemy bullet shattered one knee. Like countless others he was physically unfit to continue his army career and was honourably discharged.

It was years later before he found a job in the local dockyard. There were no pensions or financial help for the wounded soldiers at the end of the Great War. They had served their country and received their medals but were now on their own to cope with physical and emotional problems. Dad spent a lot of time with us on local walks, pointing out the various species of birds and their nesting habits, as well as the names of the stars glowing in the sky. He encouraged us to read and often read aloud to us. He was strict but fair, insisting we learn our country's history and remember our proud heritage.

My mother was a typical housewife of that era. To her a clean, tidy home was a healthy home. She made all our clothes and taught us to sew and embroider, and did not complain about the difficult Depression times when I was a child. She had a pretty voice, loved music, singing, and dancing, and over time she taught my sisters and me to enjoy the basics of ballroom dancing. My sisters and I had the usual sibling rivalries but never lost touch with each other.

We young people did not really understand what Hitler was planning in the 1930s even though Winston Churchill was forecasting what could happen if nothing were done to prevent the Nazis' attempt to take over the world. We had been warned. In 1939 we were hurled into war. Hitler continued his invasions and Britain was honour-bound to lend support to her allies. So our family registered for food and clothing coupons, and picked up gas masks along with instructions for use. Families were asked to give up their aluminum pots and pans for the war effort and the wrought-iron railings surrounding homes were removed and later melted down for munitions. Men and women trained as air raid wardens, air raid shelters were built, and those of us living close to London were issued with materials to build Anderson air raid shelters in our backyards.

The aerial bombing of Britain started almost a year later. Night and day we heard the mournful wail of sirens followed by the shattering of glass and the cries for help after the initial explosions. We groped around in the darkness amid the fires and destruction, smelling gas while choking on dust and dirt. The presence of danger and death became a part of life.

While volunteering to organize a Red Cross dance I met a soldier stationed in the local Royal Engineer barracks. We dated twice before he was posted elsewhere. We agreed to keep in touch by writing regularly each week. We did and were married within the year in Dover. Like hundreds of other young couples we did not meet again for over two years.

During this time the government announced that single young women between eighteen and twenty years of age were to be conscripted into the military services to take the place of the men sent to the fighting front. I registered, completed the necessary aptitude tests and was interviewed for military duty. After a scheduled physical examination I awaited my official call-up. It came at the beginning of 1942. I was now in the women's branch of the British army, the Auxiliary Territorial Service (ATS).

On completion of my training in Guildford, Surrey, I was ordered to accompany three other auxiliaries across London to Chelmsford, Essex. Many railway lines were damaged, making it a difficult journey. Two days later I was interviewed by an ATS officer who explained I was to accompany her to Dover to help set up a unit attached to a Royal Artillery regiment.

Dover was known Shellfire Corner and it lived up to its name. The enemy were positioned in Calais just a few miles across the English Channel. When we arrived we could not foresee the shortages of water after broken mains, or trying to keep warm when coal deliveries were delayed by enemy bombing. We spend countless hours in air raid shelters with no amenities. We were constantly exposed to the deafening noise of overhead fighter and bomber planes and to the pounding of our nearby heavy anti-aircraft guns. The torpedo sinking of Merchant Navy supply ships led to food shortages. There was also a shortage of doctors and nurses. We survived.

Victory finally came in 1945, and I was demobilized in 1946 with the rank of sergeant. My husband joined me later. Hundreds of thousands of troops had already returned home. But there were no homes. So many houses had been damaged or destroyed during the war years while none had been built.

Eventually we rented a house with friends. By 1950 we had saved enough money for the down payment on a house. With our young daughter, we moved to Rochester. Our son was born in 1951 and I was completely happy and content with our quiet life.

The big blow came in 1956. The Suez crisis. The news was not good. Newspaper headlines screamed of another war. The Egyptian president was nationalizing the Suez Canal while the governments of France and Britain wanted to control it. This conflict seemed to be of little consequence at first but suddenly there were food shortages and the prices of everything went up. My husband and his fellow workers discussed the situation and decided it would be a good idea to emigrate. Canada wanted us.

I was horrified. There was no way, no way at *all* that I would leave my beloved England. My carefree life was changing. I grudgingly read the Canadian information on emigration. Apparently my husband's firm were sending airfield equipment and parts to a place called Edmonton. So what? Let them. They were not going to send me.

Finally I agreed to go to Canada House in London for further information. We were assured that in Canada there would be immediate employment, good schooling for the children, and enjoyable weather. We eventually booked medical appointments for our physicals for the four of us. After many unhappy months I reluctantly gave way. We sold our house and furniture and booked passages on a Greek ship to take us to Canada. When the shores of England vanished, I was heartbroken.

We arrived in Edmonton in July 1957. The next weeks were a blur of activity, finding accommodation and buying basic furniture as my husband searched for work. His British qualifications were not recognized nor were his seven years of wartime service in the Royal Engineers. The union declared he required Alberta papers. It was unbelievable. With prices here much higher than at home we needed more income. It was not a matter of choice for me. I had the needed credentials and experience and had no difficulty finding employment in the office of a nearby elementary school. I was no longer a stay-at-home mother but a working mother. Fortunately I enjoyed my job with the Edmonton Public School Board, and with the help and support of staff became somewhat familiar with the curriculum. Eventually my husband acquired the necessary Alberta papers and found employment.

One immediate problem was teaching the children how to cross the road safely with the traffic travelling on the right-hand side of the street. I worried constantly that they would be involved in an accident. But they adjusted after a while. Looking back I remember my biggest challenge was trying to find out more about what the school curriculum offered. I was amazed to find there were children aged seven here in Edmonton who had not attended grade one as their admissions were strictly limited according to their birth date. Both my children were reading and writing at the age of four and had been in school by the age of five. To discover more I attended all the Home and School meetings and volunteered to act as recording secretary at each session. I met neighbours, parents, and school staff this way.

My mother, however, was distressed to hear of the brutal Edmonton winter weather. She insisted I make an appointment with the school principal to explain there was no way her grandchildren would be attending classes during the winter months. It was unsafe to be outside in the dreadfully low temperatures, she insisted. They were to be kept at home safe and warm until the weather moderated. I assured her I could buy parkas, winter boots, toques, and mittens designed to battle the cold. But I'm not sure she was completely assured we were coping. I was touched to know how concerned she was about our new life, and I must admit I smiled when I pictured her seated in her favourite spot by the fire, always there to offer advice on anything that affected her family.

In England we had owned a small, black-and-white television set since 1950. Here, TV was still a novelty in 1957. We missed the programs we had watched regularly but soon became familiar with new ones. It took time to get used to the informal way in which Canadians called each other by their first names, but eventually we realized it was a show of friendliness and acceptance.

I was often homesick and missed the sea, but my first sight of the

Rocky Mountains bonded me to them. They were so majestic, so awe-inspiring, so immense. I had never seen anything like them before. Over the years we had many visitors and have always taken them on the Edmonton, Jasper, Banff, Calgary route so they could enjoy the beauty of Alberta. Their visits here helped me keep in touch with my island home.

In 1967 my husband and I bought a home in southeast Edmonton. We still had not been back to Rochester, although we had discussed it. Finally, in 1969, I booked my first flight home alone. My husband's health was not good enough to risk his flying. When I arrived in London I stood and cried. I could see the Houses of Parliament across the river and hear Big Ben striking. These centuries-old buildings, my heritage, were intact, and I had missed them.

Surviving the brutal Alberta winters has never been easy for me. I detest snow and ice and the accompanying problems. I recall the ordeal of our first winter. We could not imagine how cold "minus" temperatures would feel, even though we would be bundled up in winter clothing. I was assured the weather here in Edmonton was healthy, as it is a dry cold. Who was I to argue?

Looking back to how distraught I was at the thought of emigration, I realize now it was partly because I am not the adventurous type. After surviving six years of war, security was paramount for me. Once here I faced the challenge of becoming assimilated, and I found volunteering was the way to meet people and become part of the community. I take writing courses and am a longtime member of the South East Seniors' Association and part of their volunteer team. I belong to the YWCA and knit warm clothing for children who need it. I continue to enjoy various trips experiencing what Canada has to offer. I take part in Remembrance Day ceremonies each year, sharing my wartime memories in various places in the city and placing at wreath at Vimy Ridge Academy to honour veterans. This day is of great importance to me.

When I go back to England I realize that although the historical buildings are still part of my heritage, social and cultural changes are apparent. I have lost many dear friends and relatives over the years and know very few of their descendants. I am now a senior. I continue to read the British news and check the London weather report daily. My love of Crown and country is as important as ever. The sight of the Union Jack flying side-by-side with the Maple Leaf flag is now, to me, a symbol of my life here in Canada.

Mary Cavill worked for the Edmonton Public School Board for thirty years before retiring from J. Percy Page High School as head secretary. In her retirement she has volunteered at the Minerva Senior Studies Institute, South East Edmonton Seniors Association, the YWCA, Vimy Ridge Academy, and J. Percy Page High School.

An avid writer, many of her wartime memoirs have been published locally and in Legion publications. She has submitted her complete wartime stories to the Dover Museum archives, and several stories to the Imperial War Museum in London, for the future use of researchers. Her freelance articles have appeared in the *Edmonton Journal*, seniors newsletters, and Remembrance Day programs.

AUGUSTINE MARAH

Hope for Africa

WRITTEN IN ALBERTA ON APRIL 3, 2004 ON THE TENTH ANNIVERSARY OF
THE RWANDA GENOCIDE

Africa, O Africa, my dear Africa
The continent of my dreams
Why are you shaped like a question
    mark?

Africa, our dear Africa, are you the
    dark continent,
or the Garden of Eden? Tell me
    Africa, who you are

Africa, mysterious Africa, why haven't you succumbed
to the heavy burdens of human trials and tribulations?

Africa, my dear Africa, where do you get your Herculean strength?

Africa, oh my dear Mother Africa
your children have been wailing for centuries
for they have been ravaged by the vagaries of time
is there any hope for your future generations?

Africa, Sweet Mother Africa

I stand in awe of your indomitable strength
in spite of all the vicissitudes of human pride,
you have remained an oasis in the desert of time.

Oh Africa, my dear Africa, you are my hope
You are my source of strength and my pride

Africa, my dear Africa, I am enchanted by your grace
for you have endured slavery, colonization, wars
famine, poverty and disease

Your children have failed to learn from you
they have failed to learn the lessons of your history
they have taken up arms against each other
they have engaged in tribal warfare and ethnic cleansing

They have massacred the innocent, the weak
and the lame, all in the name of tribal superiority
what a shame, what a self-destructive shame

Sons and daughters of Africa, don't you remember who you are?

You are God's children, so stop deceiving yourselves
with divisive labels based on an ethnicity, physical
appearance, skin colour or linguistic differences
remember that there is only one human race

Moreover, none of us mortal terrestrials had a choice
in the Almighty God's benevolent decisions
for some to be born Limba or Toutsie, Fulani or Mende
black or white, Arab or Jew

and rather than subjecting other human beings
to the worst punishment
for the least crime
of having been born different

instead, we should be celebrating
yes, celebrating the beauty in our rich and colorful diversity
So wake up from your slumber to embrace and protect
your brothers and sisters of African descent

Above all, as God's children, remember that
hope is all we have to move towards a better future
hope is not only our source of strength,
it is also our source of courage
And so, we have to have:

Hope for our continent,
and hope in ourselves
for hope is a gift from God
we should all treasure and embrace

Yes, embrace hope, as we embrace our children,
our brothers and sisters
for that is what we really are to each other
in the eyes of the Almighty God, our Creator

Africa and Children of the Diaspora

When we must endure the evil deeds of others,
hope is the only catalyst to our recovery
When life hurts due to racism or tribalism,
hope is a gift that God hands over to us

Therefore, in our not-so-perfect world,
hope is our greatest resource for a better future
a future of unity, brotherhood, progress,
of peace, harmony and serenity

Augustine Marah is an Edmonton educator and community worker. He arrived in Canada from Sierra Leone in the early 1980s to study at the University of Alberta and became president of the International Students Association. After graduating with an M.A., and teaching in local elementary, junior high, and high schools, he became the principal of the Alberta International College, a private adult education institution, from 1995 to 2005. He has served as a board member of the Edmonton Mennonite Centre for Newcomers and has been active with the Knights of Columbus. He is married with two children.

His Edmonton family grew from four to twenty on June, 15, 2000 when he welcomed sixteen relatives to the city who had fled the civil war in Sierra Leone. His church, the Assumption parish, helped to sponsor the extended family.

MAGDALENA WITKOWSKI

Two Poems

Madzia

Don't look in the mirror
You are still there
United with the lights
Of someone you love
Small and innocent
    Surrounded by dreams from
Your childhood
You might be exposed
To the world of hopelessness
Be still passionate about others
Dance with flower petals
Pushed by wind
Smile at butterflies
Find hidden fairy tales
Expand your thoughts
Run bare feet stones won't
Hurt you
Flourish your dreams
    Again and again

Jestem

Wilgoć powiek nadaje kształt miłości
Oddalenie wzbogaca uczucia.
Jestem spokojna.
Sen jest jak mgła
Dotyka lekko czubków palców
I znika w porannym oddechu.
Jestem cierpliwa.
Czuje, że pieszczę każde słowo ze słownika dojrzałych owoców
Smak mi jest bliski i znam jego wartość.
Jestem wytrwała.
Nie krzyczę, nie płaczę, nie tulę się do obcych gałęzi
Choć ich kwiaty zapachem kuszą i są tak namiętne.
Jestem mgiełką i nazywam się czekam.
Snuje się po ogrodzie i w kwiaty zaglądam.
Rozchylam ich płatki i w głąb patrzę bezwstydnie.
Jestem przelotem,
Jestem dmuchnięciem,
Jestem trwającym szczęściem,
Jestem tym kim jestem i być powinnam.

I am

TRANSLATED FROM POLISH BY MAGDALENA
WITKOWSKI WITH ANNA MIODUCHOWSKA

Moisture gathering along the eyelids gives shape to love
Partings enhance emotion.
I am calm.
Sleep is like a fog
It brushes against the tips of my fingers
And disappears in the first morning light.
I am patient.
I caress each word from the dictionary of ripe fruit
The taste is familiar and I know its worth.
I am persistent.
I neither scream nor weep, I don't embrace foreign branches
In spite of the seductive fragrance of their blossoms, their passion.
I am mist and my name is waiting.
I wander about the garden and peer into flowers.
I spread their petals and shamelessly gaze inside.
I'm here in passing,
I'm a puff of air,
I am lasting happiness,
I am longing,
I am as I am and as I should be.

Magdalena Witkowski was born in Warsaw, Poland. At the age of twelve, she discovered her passion for writing, especially poetry, a love that has never waned. She left Poland at twenty-five for adventure with a plan to explore the world. She got married in the romantic city of Paris. Her curiosity and love of freedom encouraged her to travel farther, and in 1983 she arrived in Canada, in good spirits, full of energy and dreams. Her three children, love, music, memories of childhood, times of old, and nature inspire her poetry. Her work has appeared in translation in the *Prairie Journal of Canadian Literature, Edmonton Stroll of Poets Anthology*, and is forthcoming in *NÇ D Magazine*.

The Economics of Home

In 1994, as a result of my work in the field of ophthalmology, I met a man— soon to become my husband—who had been born in Calgary and had lived in Edmonton since the age of four. Our chance meeting occurred in Phoenix, Arizona, at a contact lens/optical confer- ence. Our brief encounter was fortunate.

After months of practicing the lost art of hand-written letters, in addi- tion to nightly long-distance phone conversations, we discovered we had many other things in common: our love of the arts, our commitment to justice, our political leanings, and our connection to nature, just to name a few. But distance kept us apart; he was in Edmonton, but might as well have been on the moon given the geographical expanse between us. I was in South Carolina, in the same small town where I had been born and continued to live past my mid-forties. My children were grown, and I enjoyed a full life as an independent, single woman. I was not searching for a romantic relationship, but one came to me and provided the impetus for me to leave the place that had always been my home.

On my first trip to Canada, I arrived in Edmonton on a bitterly cold day in January. I was as moonstruck as any teenager experiencing love for the first time. Ecstatic: no other word is sufficient for what I felt. That day Drew cradled what I thought must be flowers bundled in paper. Being from a sub-tropical climate, I had never seen flowers wrapped in layers of paper. When I began tearing their protection away, he informed me, "It's thirty below outside, June . . . thirty degrees Celsius . . . below zero."

Did he say thirty below? Though he had attempted to prepare me, I was astounded. The lowest temperature I had ever experienced in South Carolina was five or six degrees below Celsius, and even that was extremely rare.

The week before my flight, during one of our telephone conversations, he had generously offered to purchase an appropriate winter coat. He had seen one, the perfect colour and size, and he was insistent that I'd need it for my visit. Independent woman that I am, I refused his offer. Thirty below and I, a born Southerner, arrived in Canada wearing only a light tapestry jacket borrowed from my sister. I didn't own a coat. After a moment of contemplation and hesitation I inquired, "Did you by any chance buy the coat you asked me about on the phone?"

"Yes. It's in my car." He was quick assure me that he'd kept the receipt, left the tags on and could return the coat if I wanted him to do so. Needless to say, I accepted his gift as graciously as possible, given my previous insistence that he not make the purchase. It was perfect. It fit, and I was ever so grateful.

My notion of the ideal temperature is thirty degrees *above* zero. One might think a ten-day January visit to Edmonton would have discouraged me from moving to the Great White North. However, people do inexplicable things under Aphrodite's irresistible spell. Love is a singular consumption; it exerts an unparalleled and incomparable influence over mind, body, and soul. Under its authority, I left a fulfilling twenty-four-year career, my family and friends and moved five thousand kilometres across the North American continent. The initial adjustment, I must admit, was difficult. However my life has been infinitely enriched in ways I could never have anticipated.

In 2004, after nine winters—the number of winters I survived was my way of measuring time—my husband and I began dividing our time between Edmonton and South Carolina. One benefit was to escape the long, cold winters, but the more important reason was to spend time with my eighty-five-year-old father, my son and daughter, grandchildren, my sister, and her family. My husband, having no children, has come to embrace my grown children and our grandchildren as his own, and they have reciprocated: another of love's blessings.

Our occupations allow us to work via the Internet. In this respect, we are fortunate, but the time is fast approaching when we will retire, and the cost of maintaining two residences will be prohibitive. It never occurred to me when I moved to Edmonton that we would retire any place other than in my small hometown. That was our original plan. But time has a way of transforming even our most strongly resolved intentions, and now I am faced with questions . . .

Where is home? Where do I belong?

For me these questions are inextricably linked to broader social and political concerns. Over the past ten years, I have become more disenchanted with the policies, foreign and domestic, of my former home country.

The issue that will affect my husband and me most significantly is the crisis in the American health-care system. The United States—by far, the richest country in the world—is the only industrialized country in the Western world that does not provide medical coverage for its citizens. I believe it is a travesty, if not criminal, for a wealthy nation to lack some type of universal health care.

If we move to the United States permanently before we turn sixty-seven, we will have to purchase private health insurance at an exorbitant cost. At age sixty-seven, we will pay monthly premiums to obtain Medicare, the coverage provided for elderly Americans. Additional insurance is necessary as Medicare covers very little of what doctors and hospitals are allowed to charge. We would have to purchase another costly policy, which would cover only some medications. Actuary computations put us in a high-risk, high-cost category even though we are both exceptionally fit and healthy. Drew has run several half-marathons, and I attend yoga and fitness classes and walk several times weekly. Even so a catastrophic illness could easily consume our entire life savings. I know this from experience in my own family.

Fifteen years ago, while attending undergraduate school, my son was diagnosed with a pituitary tumor. He has required surgery and has multiple, chronic health issues related to the grown hormone-dependent tumor, which devastated the cartilage in his large joints. Frequent medical tests and a plethora of expensive prescription drugs are required. My son has two master's degrees and has almost completed a Ph.D. in philosophy. He teaches at a university as an adjunct professor. This position provides no insurance benefits and because of his pre-existing condition, he is unable to purchase private insurance. Well over half of his annual salary is spent on the care of his health. He is just one of at least forty-seven million Americans who had no insurance last year, yet the US government spends eight billion dollars a month to pursue a highly controversial, if not down-right illegal war in Iraq.

Fortunately, Canada has a much more comprehensive system of health and social programs. We do pay higher taxes, but which is the greater burden: paying a manageable portion of your wages in exchange for the peace of mind of full protection in a health-care emergency, or paying marginally lower taxes in the US and hoping against hope that neither you nor a family member faces a health-care tsunami?

As a woman who has lived in both countries, I am more than willing to pay higher taxes in order that I and all Canadians can enjoy the benefits we are afforded by government-funded medical care. After all, citizenship is not simply an entitlement; it implies reciprocal duties, or it is an empty concept. Regardless of ethnicity, religion, or socio-economic status, the quality of health care here is the same for all. Of course, the Canadian system is far from perfect, but I believe it is a fairer system.

So again the questions come up . . .

Where is my home? Where do I belong?

These questions are not unusual. They are universal and integral to the process of discovering one's place in the world. They are essential to the never-ending lifelong pursuit of self discovery. By the age of fifty-nine, one would think I would have the answers figured out long before now.

Roman scholar and philosopher, Pliny the Elder, born in AD 23, coined the phrase "home is where the heart is"—or so we are told. This statement has been quoted so often it has become cliché. Nonetheless Pliny the Elder knew the trajectory of the human heart.

My initial decision to move to Edmonton was strictly a matter of the heart; however, my heart was divided then, as it is now. I still have a great affinity for the place of my birth: the verdant rolling landscape, its temperate climate and proximity to the beaches of the Atlantic. In some deep-rooted, inexplicable way, the town of Anderson, South Carolina— population 26,000—will always feel like my home. But Drew and I now feel compelled to make Canada our permanent home.

My life has unfolded in ways unimaginable to me on that first January day when I walked out into frigid air and experienced the wonder of sun-lit, hoarfrost-decorated trees. I have since become a Canadian citizen. I've developed a new career in writing, and I'm now in the process of a final revision of my first novel.

Edmonton's arts community has been a source of immeasurable support. The friendships I've developed here, including many with other writers, are deep and meaningful. My husband's city and his country have become home to me, although I will live here with my heart divided, always longing for a closer physical connection to family and friends in the South. I have come to the conclusion that Thomas Wolfe's observation that you can't go home again is as true and insightful as Pliny's aphorism. Home is where the heart is.

June Smith-Jeffries published her first creative work in 1998 in the anthology *Study in Grey: Women Writing about Depression*. Since that time she has published fiction, poetry, and technical articles in Canada and the United States. Among the literary journals and magazines that have published her work are *Passager Journal*, a University of Baltimore publication, *Living Our Losses* magazine, *WestWord*, *Writer's Exchange*, RSVP *Literary Press*, *Prairie Journal*, and *Captains of Consciousness Journal*. In 2002 June's entry was shortlisted in the Writers' Union of Canada Writing for Children Competition. She is currently working on her first novel, *Hope is a Fragile Thing*, which is based on her winning entry in the CBC's *Alberta Anthology* in 2003.

AHMUI CHEONG
Then and Now

Transmitted 17.24^{hr} 13.3.96 (48") 39.99

AMUI

Gemalt:
von Christiane
Langner

Propelled into the
unknown in our
iron cage!
what now,
brothers!
Ihr
bro

A little girl named Christiane drew this
portrait of Ahmui Cheong on the
eve of her departure for Canada.

Where are you from? How long have you been here? Do you like Canada?

Was it six, seven, or even eight years ago that I was first asked such questions? It used to irritate me because it didn't matter (to me) how long I'd been here. Each time I had to add another year, and another year, to my answer as time seemed to fly by.

I could not help remembering the different set of questions asked by people before I came to Edmonton.

I remember clearly the farewell party given in my honour by Ingrid.

Why were you leaving us? Were we not good enough for you? I could not help detecting some form of envy judging by the way the words were thrown at me. Some people went so far as to answer (for me): "No, she wanted to experience severe cold to get ready to climb Mount Everest." Little did they know that I wasn't that adventurous, and that I had no intention of climbing the highest mountain in the world.

That night my mind was clogged with anxiety. What could I expect from my new home, Canada? I was so overwhelmed that I could hardly hear what the other people said. I could only answer some of the simple questions.

Christiane came to my rescue. The child handed me a small drawing, which she had made of me while she was sitting quietly in a corner. Yes, that was what I looked like. And the spell was broken. I couldn't help laughing and I showed it around. I would treasure it forever, I told her.

The number of similar questions—how long have I been in Canada—will gradually increase as time goes by. After more than ten years here, I can't be bothered to add up the years anymore. However, I am amused at the creative variety of ways I am asked how long I've been here, and whether I like Canada. I guess Christiane will have to draw a different picture of me this time, as the corners of my eyes will undoubtedly crease when my face lights up with a smile.

Ahmui Cheong was born in Singapore and has lived in several different countries around the world. For those who so badly want to know, she moved to Alberta after visiting the country several times, and she likes Canada just fine.

Canadian Experience

I looked out of my window on a stormy, wintry night. The snow was blowing on the empty street ahead. Our street, called Christmas Lane every year, was decorated with bright-coloured lights and decorations.

Every mid-November, our neighbour, Greg, dubbed the Self-styled Santa, eagerly took it upon himself to remind everyone on the street that it was time to decorate for the festive season. He couldn't care about the mounting power bills, or that some seniors couldn't afford to light up so soon, or that some of us were Muslims and so Christmas had no religious significance to us.

"When in Rome, do as the Romans do," I told my family. So in the spirit of good neighbourliness, and in the spirit of Christmas, I would religiously—no pun intended—decorate my home. After all, we Muslims do not want more trouble than we already have. Those terrorists have spoiled our names and our religion enough, and I didn't want to create another international incident!

I recalled our first Christmas in Canada in 1973. We were called new Canadians then instead of Pakis. It was a proud label. "I am a new Canadian from Tanzania," I used to tell everyone in the office.

My two-year-old son, Hanif, wanted a Christmas tree. We wanted to assimilate and become true Canadians so I didn't object, but some friends heard that I, a true Muslim, planned to put a Christmas tree in my house. They were outraged. This is not in our religion or our belief, they argued. Christmas trees have nothing to do with religion, was my reply. We are now in Canada, and we should live and behave like Canadians but not forget our religion and culture. It didn't satisfy them. To each his own.

Every immigrant seeking a job in Canada has been asked at least once whether he has had Canadian experience or not. In the 1970s, it was a standard question that every employer asked in an interview. This is one commodity—Canadian Experience—that big-box stores should consider selling so that us poor immigrants can go and buy some as soon as we enter the country. Apparently, there is a huge demand for it.

During those earlier days of settlement, we, immigrants from East Africa, would all meet in the evenings, have coffee, and exchange our stories to find out if anyone was lucky enough to get a job without Canadian Experience. No such luck. Were employers using this phrase as an excuse to bar coloured immigrants out of jobs? I didn't believe it until I became a victim of Canadian Experience myself.

We arrived at our first port of call in Canada, Toronto, with only $1,000 with which to make a fresh start in our new country and with high hopes to build a great future. We were among thousands of Asians from East African countries of Tanzania, Uganda, and Kenya, who were displaced from our newly independent countries simply for being what we were—African-born but of Asian ancestry.

We were loyal to the African countries of our birth, but as it happened in Uganda, we "Asians," or "East Indians" were expelled overnight by dictator Idi Amin, creating an international outcry, which later on culminated in the largest Asian-exodus that the world had ever seen. Canada accepted six thousand Asians from Uganda alone.

In neighbouring Tanzania, Julius Nyerere had embarked upon an aggressive policy of socialism and had nationalized banks, import-export businesses and properties, which had greatly affected Asians, who were the business class. In Kenya, the Asians were also anxious to leave as majority of them were British passport holders and they were trying to get into the United Kingdom before it closed its doors to non-white immigrants. Amin's expulsion of Asians gave an added impetus to other Asians to leave Africa as they started mistrusting African leaders. It was a wake-up call for them to leave. Hence most Asian families started sending their educated and professional children abroad.

Armed with seven years of senior editorial experience and British journalism training, I arrived in Toronto thinking that getting a job would be easy. I was wrong. I went to see the managing editor of one of the dailies. Instead of looking at my resume, he chastised me for having the audacity to aspire to a job on one of "the best newspapers in Canada." He advised that I would have to work on "one of the smaller weeklies" as a start because I didn't have "Canadian experience."

I was shocked to hear this. My experience and my training were considered to be worthless. I threw him a challenge. Admittedly I lacked the so-called Canadian experience (whatever that meant) but I was prepared to work as a copy editor for a month, free of charge, and after one month all he would have to do was to tell me to go away, and I wouldn't question his decision. What I had was journalism experience and copy editing and layout skills, which were universal. I explained that I had been a copy editor on English language newspapers in Dar es Salaam and Nairobi, and I begged him to at least give me a chance.

I also mentioned to him that a British colleague who was a copy editor with me on the *Daily Nation* in Nairobi had been hired by the paper without Canadian experience! Needless to say, I didn't get the job. Fortunately, my wife was lucky and she found a position a week after our arrival.

Adjusting to life in Canada was not easy. We had come from a servant-oriented society, where Yes-Bwana (Sir), Yes-Mama (Madam), was the order of the day. There we had a servant, Juma, who also doubled as a cook, which was unusual, while our son had a full-time nanny, Elizabeth.

As a features editor of the leading English daily, I was a senior staff member and hence had the privilege of having a company-provided, two-bedroom fully furnished apartment, right in front of the Indian Ocean in a former European-only area. This was one of the fruits of *Uhuru* (independence), that we ex-colonized folks received.

In Africa, meals were always ready for memsahib, and baby Hanif was pampered from birth by our indispensable ever-present nanny until we left Dar es Salaam (Haven of Peace). When Hanif did his first "big job" in Toronto, we didn't know what to do as we had never done the "operation." We had to toss a coin to determine who was going to clean him up!

In Canada, my wife became the breadwinner, reversing the traditional role. Washing dishes, cleaning the house, picking up and dropping off Hanif from the day care, became my chores as the house-husband. In my search for a job, my strategy was to go to a Greyhound bus station every morning, pick an Ontario city and present myself to the newspaper office to see the managing editor of the newspaper. Most of the time I would succeed in seeing the managing editor or the editor, drop off my resume and indicate to him that I was available for work. I was willing to go any-where where I could find a position. In this regard I had seen managing editors of London, Ontario; Kitchener, Waterloo, Guelph, Windsor, and Peterborough, apart from talking to major metro Toronto weeklies.

At that time the head office of Southam newspapers, which then owned thirteen major dailies across Canada, was in Toronto. The guy in charge was a pleasant young Jewish fellow who became quite sympathetic to my plight. He interviewed me and sent my resume to some Southam papers. I heard from two of them: Edmonton and Winnipeg, and both offered me positions. I chose Edmonton as they offered slightly more money than Winnipeg. That's how I ended up at the *Edmonton Journal* in March 1973.

Working on a Canadian daily had its ups and downs. There were people who were very friendly and there were some who were not so friendly, and one had to tread skillfully between them. Having worked at two English dailies in East Africa, I had no problem working on the copy desk and I got used to the system in no time.

While still a newcomer to Edmonton, I had the privilege to be appointed chairman of Shia Ismaili Muslim community, followers of His Highness the Aga Khan. The appointment, which is voluntary, is considered to be quite prestigious by members of the community, as the Aga Khan makes it. In this capacity, I had to oversee the settlement of Ugandan refugees who had just arrived and look after the general welfare of other members of the community. This placed a strain on my personal life as a new immigrant myself trying to get settled. However, with the help and dedication of other volunteers and members of my committee, I was able to discharge my duties successfully for seven years. The crowning glory of my term came when the Aga Khan paid the first visit to Edmonton, which my wife and I had the privilege to host in 1979.

As far as my career was concerned, I always wanted to own my own newspaper. In 1976 I accepted a position as associate publisher of *Bonnyville Nouvelle*, a long established weekly in northeastern Alberta. This was the boom time when Imperial Oil had just announced its $2 billion Cold Lake heavy oil project, and the region was prosperous. Without any modesty, I can say that the paper gained prestige and editorial excellence in its coverage under my supervision and with my previous daily newspaper experience.

Having never worked on a weekly in my life, this job became an excellent training ground and prepared me for my life's ambition of buying my own paper in 1979. We had zeroed in on our choice as we wanted to buy a paper within commuting distance of Edmonton or Calgary. We got our wish when we heard that two papers were available: *Airdrie Echo* and *Morinville Mirror*. Our first choice was *Airdrie Echo* since it was bigger and more established. My wife also had relatives in Calgary. We put in an offer on the asking price and it was accepted, but unfortunately while the lawyers were drawing up the papers, a better offer, more than the asking price, was placed on the table with the result that we lost the Airdrie deal.

We went after our second choice, the *Morinville Mirror*, which was losing money at the time. Over our accountant's objections, we bought it. I had full confidence in myself that I would turn the paper around. We transformed it from a rag into a professionally produced, readable product. In just about a month, the business community saw the difference and began to support the paper by advertising in it instead of in the two competitors, one from St. Albert and another from Westlock, both of which were freely circulated in our area.

Another strategy we adopted was to hire an advertising salesman with specific instructions to make calls to Edmonton car dealerships, furniture stores, and other businesses in the west and northern parts of the city. This became very appealing to advertisers as our papers serviced most commuting towns and villages throughout the County of Sturgeon.

We always had two full-time reporters on staff, apart from advertising sales, production, layout, and front office staff. The tables were turned now. The former employee was now sitting in the employer's chair. I was now hiring people and many times I felt like asking applicants if they had Canadian experience, especially those who were straight from colleges and universities, but I never succumbed to the temptation.

In 1980 we established the *Redwater Tribune*, serving the northeastern part of the County of Sturgeon. By then circulation of the *Mirror* was 6,934 while *The Tribune* was 5,448. My wife and I did our best to survive in one of the most competitive markets in Alberta and successfully published our two papers for twenty-five years. It wasn't easy. The competitors used every trick they could to push us out of business. They offered incentives to advertisers and used every gimmick in the trade, but we ploughed ahead, determined to succeed until we celebrated our twenty-fifth anniversary.

When I look back, I see a thirty-six-year-old courageous young man confidently walking into a French-Canadian town, not knowing anyone, and investing all of his life's savings in a losing business. I also see a stupid, non-white young man trying to establish himself in a community where the acceptance of other cultures was questionable. As soon as it became known that I had purchased the paper, it was brought to my attention that my ancestry and race were being questioned in "certain quarters." Fortunately, most people in the community received us well, and, as they began knowing us, there were no ugly incidents to speak of.

One of our competitors predicted that we wouldn't last, in his words, "more than six months." Unfortunately, for him, we gave him a tough time, with support from our advertisers, for more than two decades. In May 2005 we sold the papers to Sun Media's subsidiary, Bowes Publishers, Canada's second largest publishing group, which publishes several weeklies in metro Edmonton. As publisher and editor of these two weeklies, I was satisfied that the papers needed the economic muscle of a chain to take them to their next level of economic growth and advancement, and that the weekly newspaper industry had reached a stage where it was going to be difficult, if not impossible, for independent publishers like myself to operate. It was time to say good-bye, so long, *au revoir*, to Morinville from the Ladhas!

The future of these papers looks bright as I settle in my favourite chair, behind my computer, to begin writing that autobiographical book that I always contemplated writing. Stay tuned.

Mansoor Ladha lives in Calgary and freelances for the *Calgary Herald* and *Vancouver Sun*. His book, *A Portrait in Pluralism: Aga Khan's Shia Ismailis Muslims*, was published in March 2008.

WILMA RUBENS
Adventure Assured

*There is something I notice
about desire, that it opens
the eyes and
strikes us blind at the same
time.*
—Jane Smiley

In the beginning, a dream looks alluring, like a spider's web glistening in the early morning sun. The spider silently waits for its unsuspecting prey.

In the six years I lived in Sydney, Australia—far from snowy mountains—the steaming eucalypts, magenta bougainvillea, raucous cockatoos, my friendly neighbours and inspiring colleagues seduced me into a comfortable lifestyle while my crampons rusted in the humid basement. As a busy mother of two, Chris and Shona, I had little time to pine after wild places far from the rumble of city traffic. I suppressed my vivid memories of my life before children, of the silent snow, the crunch of glacier ice under my crampons, and the magnetic pulse of mountain summits.

Twenty years previously, just after the winter solstice, I had pursued my husband across the heather moors under low Scottish clouds. It was our common love of mountains that provided the glue for our enduring relationship. Our passion lured us from our beloved Scotland to Afghanistan, Kashmir, Pakistan, Oman, New Zealand, and Australia. Places that sometimes made me feel I was living in the pages of *National Geographic*. I loved the warm-hearted Ozzies but there were no tall-glaciated mountains on that surf-fringed red continent.

One warm September afternoon, my children were playing with friends in their tent by the pink oleanders in our backyard when five-year-old Chris picked up the phone.

"It's Dad, he wants to speak to you."

My husband Clive, without preamble, asked, "Do you want to go and live in Calgary? The company has offered me a transfer."

Juggling the pots on the stove, and with three-year-old Shona clinging to my leg, I mumbled, "I don't know. It's so cold there. We are only just settling into this house. We've been here just over a year."

Many times over the next few weeks Clive and I walked along the sandy pathways of Sydney's beautiful coastal parks through hairpin banksias, pink begonia bushes, and flannel flowers. Above the growl of the surf we discussed the pros and cons of an international move with our young family.

"It feels like we have only just settled into our new house. The kids love the pool," I said. "How can we even think of moving again?"

"Well, I know it would be hard but we have always grabbed opportunities," Clive replied. " The company will cover all the moving charges. It will be easier than last time. It would be good for my career."

"What do you mean last time? It was so exciting to move to India then Oman. But remember how I really struggled when we left Scotland and moved to New Zealand?"

"I thought you loved New Zealand. You kept talking about how much you missed your Kiwi friends and the mountains when we moved to Sydney."

Clive challenged me, and I tried to explain. "I did love New Zealand. When I moved here it was hard to be pregnant. I didn't know anyone.

The city seemed so flat and the traffic so busy. I missed the mountains. Now I have made great friends and neighbours, and I have just started teaching conflict resolution. I would miss all the support from the Conflict Resolution Network," I continued, impatiently. "And Chris is just about to start school, which is just around the corner. Remember that was one of the reasons we bought this house. That was only fifteen months ago."

"I still have a job here," Clive said. "We don't need to go." But he wouldn't quite let go of the idea. "You know how stretched we are financially. The mortgage rate has increased from 12 per cent to 18 per cent in six months. This might be an opportunity to get ahead financially."

"I know that," I countered. "Still I love this house I can't begin to think about selling it."

"We could rent it out," he said. "Maybe we are just getting stuck in our ways. Remember how beautiful the Rocky Mountains were when we visited Canada last year? You can see them from Calgary. We could go skiing again and take the kids." By now I was remembering how much I had loved to ski in New Zealand.

"It is only an eight-hour flight to Scotland from Calgary," Clive reminded me. "Chris and Shona could get to know Scotland, their cousins and grandparents." He had a point, there. I did miss my sisters and their families. "But the weather sounds awful," I said. "It was minus 20 today in Calgary and plus 20 here. We must be crazy even to think about moving."

Clive wasn't giving up yet. "Imagine: Calgary has only half a million people. Compared to four million here in Sydney. The traffic here is so congested."

I interrupted him with a painful truth: "You know it will be easier for you. You will just move from one office to another. I will have to start my life all over."

Clive was as confused as me. "I don't know what we should do. Still if we work hard we can make sure when we arrive in Calgary we will catch the ball in the air and fly with it."

It was a tumultuous time. One day we were going and the next day we had decided it was too overwhelming, and we'd stay.

In January 1990 a huge moving container rolled up to the house. Chris, Shona, and I watched sadly as their beloved toys and our entire household belongings were packed tightly inside. I tried to explain that they were going on a ship to Calgary while we were flying. We left Sydney in torrential rain. It was as if the weather was expressing the feelings I was unable to unlock. We landed in Canada to our first Calgary blizzard and drove from the airport on ice-covered roads. We spent a chaotic week in Calgary, bought a house, skates, long underwear, snow boots, hats, gloves. We skied at Canada Olympic Park. Skiing with two young kids was not quite like the vision of the happy family I had imagined on a ski hill some months before.

A short time later, we were excited to take the children for their first visit to Scotland to meet their cousins, aunts and uncles and grandparents. After three weeks constrained in my mother-in-law's apartment, filled with its antique plates and teapots, with damp Scottish winter and warm Scottish hospitality, I was ready to return to Sydney, my warm backyard, friendly neighbours and colleagues, back to the known and the familiar.

All too soon we returned to Calgary's desolate wintry landscape to start a new chapter in our lives. We joked that we had exiled ourselves to the frozen tundra. How different could two places be? Australia had nine months of hot humidity with winter temperatures of ten degrees below zero. In Calgary, they said, there were nine months of winter and three months of poor sledding.

Oh yes, I did speak English although I did not speak Canadian. My words were often misunderstood. I asked about curtains not drapes, pavements not sidewalks, bonnets not trunks, toilets not washrooms. I didn't know anybody. The kids got chicken pox. One day—sick, cold, and disoriented—I parked the car downtown to do an errand and when I returned with my two little kids, the car had vanished. Towed to the pound. Ten days later I was back at the airport waving my husband goodbye. In his position as International Exploration manager he was frequently away on international business in the oil industry. I was left unsupported in a cold and unfamiliar city.

I hit an all time low when I took my five-year-old to school. That night the phone rang. "I am Mrs. Brown, the kindergarten teacher. Your son kicked me today. We don't do that here." Humiliated I swallowed back my tears.

Will I ever forget the blizzards in the first winter, with snow shrieking past my windows horizontally? I thought to myself: "If the roof blows off we will all die!" After living in our new house for a month I felt uneasy. What was the matter with me? Then I realized that my windows had been open wide all year round for six years. In Calgary they were closed tight to keep out the extreme cold. I was amazed at the tenacity of Canadians who never let the extreme weather interfere with their plans.

I had let go of the riverbank of life, all that was familiar. I was out in the current, drowning. Every once in a while I raised my head above the swirling waters and gulped some air before sinking in the chaotic flow. Although I adored our escape weekends to the mountains, I soon decided I was not fond of sprawling Calgary. In those first months I was certain I wanted to go back to my pleasant life in Sydney.

My embryonic career as a conflict resolution consultant was lost in the move. I did not feel comfortable burdening my new acquaintances with my wildly fluctuating emotions. I talked to a counsellor and spoke of my confusion. Moving from one hemisphere to another I had literally turned my life upside down. "Your life is your career," she told me kindly. I found comfort in her words. "You are the kingpin of your family." Rather than try and sort out my whole life, all at once, I "chunked it." First organize the house. Next, settle children into their routine. Then enjoy a little mountain climbing, and eventually resume a career. One small piece at a time.

The parks in Calgary felt like wastelands, the leafless trees, stark against the ice-blue sky anchored in the frozen ground. One day, driving around, tears streaming down my face, I had a chat with myself.

You are here for better or for worse. You know from previous experiences that if you continue to find it hateful, it will be hateful. What can you begin to like?

I looked out of the car window into the vast Alberta skyscape. I could begin to love the bulbous clouds, clean air, and the sunshine. I could begin to love the soft curve of the blonde hillside on Nose Hill. I could begin to appreciate the school system that taught young children about negotiation.

That first spring when the ice melted I kissed the delicate purple crocuses as they rose miraculously from the brown earth. Once the children were asleep, in my treeless garden, I dug deep holes in the earth. Stubbornly I hacked at the solid river clay with a crowbar to excavate the large rocks. I planted four lodgepole pines, a silver birch, and a mountain rowan. There was a recognizable familiarity in the long evenings. After thirteen years in the southern hemisphere the northern air rekindled warm memories of my Scottish homeland. Assisted by the alchemy of the cool dusk around my face, with Canadian dirt embedded under my fingernails, I began to root myself in Alberta.

The birthing pains of creating a new life for my young family and myself in the unfamiliar territory of North America continued. I returned to the counsellor. "You look so sad," she said. Her words shocked me. I had no idea someone could read my emotions from my face. I felt naked and vulnerable. Later one summer evening, the kids tucked up in bed, my husband in some far-off place looking for oil, I followed her suggestion, lit a candle, and began to write.

I wrote about missing the warmth of the Australian sun, the tall trees, the yellow wattles, the crashing ocean on Manly Beach, sailing with balmy sea breezes, my close friends, the kindergarten my kids had attended, the Conflict Resolution Network where I had found support and stimulation for my career. I wrote about the move from New Zealand to Australia, how I missed the wonderful friendships I had made in New Zealand, mountains before children, striding over airy ridges in the Southern Alps. Three tear-stained pages later I hit the bottom of my emotional turmoil. Sobbing, I remembered how three months after I had moved to New Zealand from Britain, I was called from my science classroom, and escorted by an old nun to a small telephone booth in a dark corridor in the bowels of the Sacred Heart Convent. My husband was on the other end of the phone, gently telling me my mother had been killed in a car accident. That northern summer night in Calgary, twelve years later the dam broke, and grief that had been firmly locked inside was released.

Letting go, peace followed. At forty-two I began to understand the ebb and flow of my emotions.

Our first Canadian summer holiday came, and we set out to explore our new country. We marvelled as we drove through Kootenay National

Park to Invermere. Restless and wandering we found ourselves camping in Kokanee Creek Provincial Park outside Nelson, British Columbia. I was surrounded by the peaceful presence of the tall cedar trees. Swimming in the warm lake, the children happily digging in the sand, I knew all would be well. I could make it in this new land.

To help us embrace the long cold winters we joined the Sunshine Ski Club. The club was the one place where we were known as a family. Each Sunday we'd trek up to Sunshine Village to enjoy the camaraderie of other families who liked to ski. My young children loved to meet their friends and race down the mountain. Little did I know then that both of them would pursue careers in the ski industry—my daughter now an Olympian on the Canadian Ski Team and my son an extreme skier for Matchstick Productions.

And now it is springtime, eighteen years later. After another move, this time to Canmore, in the mountains, I write under the glistening snows of the Big Sister. New leaves on the aspens uncurl like green rosebuds.

I reflect on what I have learned. It was easy to change my external world when I moved to a new place, but I carried inner baggage wherever I travelled. I have discovered that major external change amplifies my internal turmoil. This forces me to explore the interior recesses of myself, to unravel my fears, my needs, and my unconscious motivation. I have learned how to listen to my inner demons and retrieve their wisdom with patience and kindness. Following my dreams in a new country holds many challenges and exciting possibilities. While it may be a roller-coaster ride, adventure is assured and the rewards priceless.

Wilma G. Rubens is a published writer and a conflict resolution facilitator. She writes to make sense of her diverse life experiences. Born in Scotland, she has lived all over the world and currently resides in Canmore, Alberta. She has two grown children and a husband who have been known to test her conflict resolution skills. She adores the Rocky Mountains. She sometimes says her biggest achievement is to have thrived through seventeen Canadian winters.

Escaping the Cage

I was once a bird trapped in a cage with no one to turn to but myself. I waited impatiently, day after day, to somehow escape so that I could flee to the outside world. I imagined that the outside life would be filled with freedom, adventure, and love. I knew that once I finally discovered the courage that was buried deep within my soul, I would never go back to that dark and rusty cage; freedom was something I wanted so badly.

I was born in 1946, a war-torn age when Lebanon had to overcome its strife. Poverty crept into all corners of our village; everyone had been in pain and so badly wanted a normal life. We imagined the kind of life that existed in North American households; a father would come home after work to his beautiful wife and children and enjoy a lavish meal. We wanted that life, that family, and that feeling of freedom, which was so hard to reach. It was as if we were small children trying to get to a cookie jar.

That's what the North American life was like: a jar of warm delicious cookies, high up on a counter and hard to reach. It was up to me to reach that jar, and being the persistent, stubborn individual I am, I strived to get it because I wouldn't settle for anything else. I wanted to get out of Lebanon so badly that I was obsessed about my departure and dreamt about it night and day. It was only time that separated me from my escape.

School was an important aspect in my life. I believed then, and still do, that when you have an education, you can unlock the door to success. Luckily, I had a key to unlock the door. As a young man, I received a scholarship to study abroad in Greece. I planned to attend a monastery and study theology. My parents were upset when I had told them of my plans, but they understood deep down that there would be no future for me in Lebanon. Leaving my country, my parents, and my way of life in Lebanon was not an easy choice, but I had to do it.

When I was studying in Greece, I often felt depressed and lonely. I missed my family so much. Although my living situation was better and I was in a beautiful country, I so badly missed hearing the voices of my loved ones. A few times, due to the stress of my new surroundings and my homesickness, I found myself on the brink of leaving everything I had in Greece to return to Lebanon. Eventually I made many friends, and slowly, but surely, I began to feel at home. I decided to continue my studies in Greece.

A year later I received another scholarship to study theology at St. Vladimir's Seminary in New York City. I accepted the scholarship so that I could continue my journey as an academic. When I arrived in New York, Archbishop Phillip Saliba welcomed me, and I had dinner with him. I encountered a problem; he was speaking in English with me instead of Arabic. I couldn't understand him at all. He advised me to go to Los Angeles to one of his churches there to enroll in a private language school. So for six months I assisted a priest in Los Angeles during the day and I attended English classes at night. After six months, the parish priest phoned the archbishop and told him that I was able to enroll in St. Vladimir's Seminary without any difficulties and continue my studies.

Soon enough, I received my master's degree in theology. While in

New York, I decided to continue my education by pursuing my bachelor of arts degree at Adelphi University. Gaining my theology degree was conditional of my completing my undergraduate degree. After all of my education was completed, I was ordained and transferred to serve at a church in Edmonton, Alberta, called St. Philip's Antiochian Orthodox Church. I focused my ministry on education, culture, and spiritual formation.

The same year, in 1981, I had met someone who would change my life forever. Her name was Vera, and she was one of the parishioners at St. Philip's. Vera was the sweetest lady I had ever met, and her friendliness helped me overcome a lot of my nervousness since I was new to Edmonton and uncertain. Years and years passed. Vera remained the sweet lady she had been when I first met her, but by then I had started to feel something more for her. I knew I was in love for the first time. Every time I talked with Vera, or simply caught a glimpse of her, I had a rush of butterflies in my stomach. Weeks passed, and all I could think of was her. I finally asked her if she wanted to go out for dinner. Being the sweetheart she is, she accepted my offer. After two years of dating, I proposed to her. I couldn't have asked for a more perfect experience in life than the day she accepted my proposal. On July 1, 1988, Vera and I exchanged our sacred vows in the church where I had been serving.

Life was amazing for me, and I was convinced it couldn't get better. I had everything I could possibly wish for: a beautiful wife, a rewarding career, and a countless friends. Although I was happy beyond belief, there was a small void within me and it was within my wife, too. We were content with our lives but we wanted something more, we wanted a baby. One year and one month after we got married, we had a gorgeous baby girl named Michelle Alexandra. Life was truly perfect because of the gift we had been given from above.

Now I am here, twenty-six years later, still in Edmonton because I know this is where I truly belong. I have found my home here in this amazing country, the country that gave me freedom and a life I am so very grateful for. I am still a priest, serving the Canadian Orthodox community, and I also work for the government as an interpreter for the Arabic and Greek languages. Recently, I have began to translate a story in Arabic, written by George Zaidan, called *The Girl of Ghassan*, for the *Canadian Arab News,* a newspaper here in Edmonton. I wanted to reach out to the younger generation here who might not be familiar with popular Arabic literature of the past. Every single edition has a chapter of the story. Being involved with the Arabic community is very important to me because it allows me to connect to my cultural roots. My wife and daughter have never been better; Vera is the manager of a women's boutique and Michelle is going to college working hard to get her bachelor of science degree.

Every day I wake up and thank God for all the gifts he has given me. I was once a bird trapped in a cage with nowhere to go, but I was blessed to find the key to get out. I will never forget where I came from, or the struggles I had to overcome to attain the life that I wanted so badly. Many times I was uncertain about where I was going and which path I should take, but fortunately I was blessed with a plan of action. God had given me instructions on how to live my life, and I have devoted my body and soul to his cause.

I remember dreaming in Lebanon about the perfect life that the media depicted. I can honestly say that my life has been even better than the one I craved when I was young. I have everything and more, perhaps, because I worked so hard to get what I wanted. I am glad that I was finally given a chair so that I could reach up to the cookie jar; the cookies tasted better than I expected!

Reverend Father Basil Solounias is a Canadian Orthodox priest at St. Stephen's in Edmonton. In his spare time, for his own pleasure, he has worked to translate the romantic historical fiction of a prolific writer George, or Jirji, Zaidan, (1861–1914) from Arabic into English. He hopes to find a publisher for his translation of *The Girl of Ghassan.*

SUDHIR JAIN

From Sahara Desert to Alberta Prairie in Four Interviews

1.

A lot happened to me during the first six years of the 1960s. I left India on a slow boat for England, got a post-graduate degree in geology, secured my first job, married a cute English girl, and moved to North Africa with her. Evelyn and I spent five prime years of our lives in the Mediterranean port of Tripoli in the Kingdom, later the Arab Republic, of Libya. It is a picturesque city sandwiched between the beautiful blue sea in the north and barren boundless Sahara desert to the south. My work in the exploration department of a large American oil company was not strenuous, and it was quite well paid. For the first time in our lives we felt affluent because what we could not afford did not stare at us from the store windows. The pace of life was slow, and after the hectic time in England we felt an aura of peace had surrounded us.

Still, all was not a smooth sailing. The reverie was interrupted, albeit for brief periods, on two occasions by world-shattering events. Births of our daughters may have played a part in triggering both of them. One week before the due date of the first daughter, Israel attacked the Arab countries on its borders and caused a panic in our expatriate community. My employer ordered the evacuation of all spouses and children, pregnant Evelyn included. As a result, Sarah was born in far from ideal conditions in England, and her father had an interminable wait to cuddle her till she arrived in Libya at the ripe old age of six weeks.

Two and a half years later, a month before our second daughter Kamini was due, junior officers in the fledgling Libyan army replaced the King with the Revolutionary Command Council, consisting of themselves. The result was a curfew that lasted several months. Fortunately, the baby was born by induction and the hospital visits and the birth could be arranged in permitted hours. In spite of these upheavals, and some minor inconveniences like having to move house a few times by government order and living through the wind storms that dumped on Tripoli all the sand the desert could spare, life there was relaxed and pleasant. The sun, sand, and the sea provided excellent environment for Sarah and Kamini and our international social circle and frequent vacations to exciting tourist destinations provided plenty of recreation.

However, like all good things do, the happy expatriate life came to an end. Politics brought petroleum exploration to a halt, and with a heavy heart and some nervousness we decided to move.

We couldn't return to Evelyn's England or my India for several practical reasons. Therefore, we applied for visas to the United States and Canada with the intention of going to the country that granted us the papers first. I mailed the Canadian application to the nearest embassy in France and visited the US consulate in Tripoli. A friendly officer asked me to fill up some forms. He examined them in private and then interviewed me. I don't remember the details but do remember the consul as a kindly man not much older than me. His last words were, "You are a person of special merit. We need people like you. The necessary papers will be in the mail within a few weeks."

The Green Card, permission for the family to live and work in the Promised Land of America, duly arrived in a couple of months. About the same time, the Canadian consulate invited the whole family, including three-year-old Sarah and one-year-old Kamini, to an interview in Marseilles, France. The letter emphasized that there was no guarantee our application would be approved. The divergent responses from the two countries left us only one option, America. Our American friends considered our decision to leave a good job and move to the New World, with no assured job, daring in our presence and utterly foolish behind our backs. They knew that the oil industry back home was in a slump and the job prospects were dim. But I was young and brash and felt in my bones that my special skills would land me a job in no time. Evelyn was nervous but supportive. My employer and a number of other major oil companies had their exploration departments in Dallas, Texas. Both of us had spent some time there. We booked flights to that city with a three-day stopover in Philadelphia to visit Evelyn's two uncles.

2.

The uncles greeted us at the airport. The older brother was a widower in his sixties. His home was in a rundown part of Philadelphia that was fashionable when he had acquired the property thirty years before. The younger sibling was a bachelor in his fifties who lived in an apartment a few miles away in New Jersey. We stayed in Philadelphia because it was convenient for sightseeing. The uncles were gracious hosts. They treated us kindly. They escorted us to the Liberty Bell with its prominent crack; to Ben Franklin's famous home; to Bertram's garden, supposedly the first garden in America; and to the home of Betsy Ross, who stitched the first American flag and shared the family name with Evelyn. In the evening they regaled us with the family history Evelyn was not familiar with.

The largest company in aerial surveying was located in this "city of brotherly love." My postgraduate studies were vaguely related to this line of business although the work experience was in a different area. Evelyn suggested calling them to see if there was a job opening. The receptionist put me in touch with Ron Hartman, the chief surveyor. He was impressed by my qualifications and offered to interview me for a position in Algeria. I was dumbstruck. When my senses returned I pointed out that returning to the country next door to the one we had left only three days earlier was not an appealing proposition. He did not understand my viewpoint but invited me to see their facilities anyway. I accepted, thinking that there might be some need for their services if I joined an oil company. It would be useful to know the extent of their abilities.

The company was located in a residential area that was upscale before the recent mass movement of middle class to the suburbs. Ron Hartman showed me round and introduced me to his colleagues. When we were reviewing some maps, an elderly gentleman shuffled in leaning on a stick and squinting as if the light was hurting his eyes.

"Who is he?" asked the old man.

"Dr. Hermann Ackerman, let me introduce you to Dr. Sudhir Jain, he has just come from Libya," said Ron.

"Sudhir Jain, of Roy and Jain fame?" Hermann looked questioningly at me, referring to an obscure paper I had co-authored ten years earlier.

"Yes sir, Ackerman of Ackerman and Dix, I presume," I replied referring to a celebrated paper of thirty years before. This must have pleased the old master. He turned to Ron, "What is he doing here?"

"Looking for a job," Ron replied.

"What are you waiting for? Hire him. He will solve all your problems." With these fateful words Hermann disappeared into a cubbyhole nearby.

Ron offered me a job that included a significant component of research and development. That suited me to a T. An hour later, I was boasting to Evelyn that I had secured a job on the first working day after arriving in a country in the middle of a recession. She was relieved although not happy with the salary.

3.

We settled down in a rented home in suburban Bucks County. After a year, we bought in a Sheriff's auction a palatial home nearby, which we could afford only because it needed a thorough renovation. With the help of my kind colleagues and a lot of hard work by Evelyn we completed the job within our tight time frame and limited budget. There were still things to be done on the outside, and we proceeded with them after moving in as the time permitted. It was three months to the day when Evelyn put the brushes away after painting the outside. The same evening, a call came from Calgary.

"Would you be interested in managing research for a small company with big ambitions?" I looked up Calgary on the map and casual enquiries revealed that it was the oil capital of Canada. Thinking that there was no harm in interviewing the company, I took the first Friday in November off on a phony pretext and flew to meet my next employer.

The view from the plane was interesting. Gold colours of autumn changed to the brown of early winter as the plane crossed into Ontario. The scenery became somewhat monotonous west of Ontario; small hamlets dotted the bald prairie here and there under a thick blanket of snow. The plane circled over downtown Calgary before landing. The bright lights of the city were impressive, in view of brownouts common in the American cities, but the downtown area had only a handful of tall buildings other than a tower.

The tiny airport confirmed the small size of the city. Yet the cab driver managed to get lost while taking me to the home of the Mahoneys, our friends from Libya who had come to Canada about the time we had moved to the US. They told me how much they enjoyed living in what looked to me a godforsaken city in the frozen tundra. They assured me that it was hardly ever this cold; I had the misfortune of arriving there on the coldest November day on record. They showed me the equipment for winter recreation, downhill and cross-country skis, skates, and snowshoes, and the necessities for survival like thick parkas, which kept them warm when it was forty degrees below zero.

Next morning, the problems of living in Calgary were brought home. The engine froze and Mahoneys' car refused to budge. I called a cab and got to the interview an hour late. The prospective employer was most understanding. He showed me around, checked my credentials, and offered me the job. Saying the taxes and the cost of living were high in Canada, he set the salary at a significantly higher level than I had suggested.

Pleased as punch I flew home the next day. It was middle of the night when I slipped into bed. Evelyn opened one eye and asked, "How did it go?"

"Calgary is a very clean city," I replied.

The company called to confirm our understanding and advised me to visit the Canadian consulate in New York the following Monday. After waiting for an appropriate duration, we were ushered into the elegant office of the consul. The room was decorated with the pictures of old men not known to us. The interview was short and to the point.

"Will you learn French?" the esteemed official asked in heavily French-accented English.

"I am going to Calgary, Alberta," I replied. "Every one speaks English there."

"Canada is a bilingual country, you know." The consul was eager to enlighten me.

"I already speak three languages, and learning another is not my top priority," I said honestly, but as it turned out, foolishly. Strange though it may seem, the two often go together.

"It will take five years or more for your turn to arrive. Hopefully they will keep the job open for you." The consul stood up to escort us to the door.

Evelyn was secretly pleased at this rebuff. It had taken her two years of hard work to break down the doors of the social fortress common in established cities, and she was feeling settled at last. She had agreed to move reluctantly when I went down on my knees and told her with folded hands how important the promotion was to me. The gods were on her side for once but she did not gloat. Like a good wife of ten years standing, she consoled me and pointed out the possibility of a promotion in my current company.

I called Calgary to inform them of the consul's final words.

"Don't worry we will look after it," they said. The words played on my ear drums after a two-thousand-mile journey over telephone lines.

A week later, the minister's permit arrived. Two months later, we were in the driveway of the Mahoney residence in Calgary. It was a cold day, the coldest February day on record, if you still believe in such pronouncements. It was pitch dark at four in the afternoon. Our daughters disappeared into the snow bank as they hopped out of the cab, but expert shovelling by the driver got them out in the nick of time. This experience must have made a lasting impression; both of them moved to warmer climes as soon as they became adults. As for Evelyn and me, I must have exceeded the level of my competence. No company offered another job and we settled down to a sedentary life in a self-proclaimed cow town. I never learned to skate or ski, but being a masochist, I did learn to enjoy freezing in the dark while counting my blessings on my shivering fingers.

Sudhir Jain is a retired geophysicist. He lives in Calgary with his wife who practices medicine. They have three adult daughters. Jain immigrated to England from India at the age of twenty-three and then moved to Libya and the United States before settling in Canada thirteen years later. He has published forty technical papers and hundreds of letters on a wide variety of subjects in local, national, and international newspapers and magazines. He wrote a monthly column in *Lakeview News* for two years and weekly freelance columns on the *Globe and Mail* website during the 2004 elections for Canada's parliament. His stories have been read on CBC Radio and essays published in the *Globe and Mail*. A collection of his stories, *Isolde's Dream and Other Stories*, was published in 2007. Another book, provisionally titled *Pages from an Immigrant's Diary*, is currently being reviewed by a publisher.

Linda Goyette is an Edmonton writer, editor, and journalist with an interest in oral history and contemporary storytelling in Alberta. Her previous books for adults include: *Standing Together: Women Speak Out About Violence and Abuse*; *Second Opinion*, a collection of her journalism; and *Edmonton In Our Own Words*, for which she won the Grant MacEwan Author's Award in 2005. Her books of Alberta stories for children include *Rocky Mountain Kids* and *Kidmonton: True Stories of River City Kids*.